DRAGON DEFENDING

DRAGON DEFENDING

DRAGON APPARENT™ BOOK SEVEN

TALIA BECKETT

DISRUPTIVE IMAGINATION

DON'T MISS OUR NEW RELEASES

Join the LMBPN email list to be notified of new releases and special promotions (which happen often) by following this link:

http://lmbpn.com/email/

This book is a work of fiction. All of the characters, organizations, and events portrayed in this novel are either products of the author's imagination or are used fictitiously. Sometimes both.

Copyright © 2023 Talia Beckett
Cover by Bandrei
Cover copyright © LMBPN Publishing

LMBPN Publishing supports the right to free expression and the value of copyright. The purpose of copyright is to encourage writers and artists to produce the creative works that enrich our culture.

The distribution of this book without permission is a theft of the author's intellectual property. If you would like permission to use material from the book (other than for review purposes), please contact support@lmbpn.com. Thank you for your support of the author's rights.

LMBPN Publishing
PMB 196, 2540 South Maryland Pkwy
Las Vegas, NV 89109

Version 1.00 May, 2023
eBook ISBN: 979-8-88541-782-2
Print ISBN: 979-8-88878-388-7

THE DRAGON DEFENDING TEAM

Thanks to my JIT Team:

Dorothy Lloyd
Christopher Gilliard
Jeff Goode
Diane L. Smith
Paul Westman

DEDICATION

To Bryan. Somehow you have an endless patience for the thoughts in my head, the chaos in my life from all its many sources and you look at me through it all the way I hope Neritas looks at Scarlet.
I hope we're always fighting the demons of life alongside each other.

— Talia

CHAPTER ONE

The world had changed so fast in a short time. I looked out over the crowd that had gathered, able to see them without them being able to see me. It was scary. Politicians, soldiers, cops, and so many reporters that they'd needed to get a bigger tent to hold them all.

The people in charge of the US wanted to keep the dragons contained, so the tent had been set up in a clearing near the side of the road not that far from Detaris, the dragon capital city of the world.

I was the dragon queen, but it hadn't been a clear route to the throne. Until six months ago I hadn't even known I was a dragon, let alone royalty.

And the demon I was meant to protect the world from had escaped. Three days ago.

I'd barely slept the night before and had woken up in a pile of tangled limbs with Flick and Neritas. We hadn't intended to share the bed, but none of us had been able to sleep. After the conversation we'd had, it had gotten worse.

I'd finally told Flick that Neritas had somehow developed the same magical ability as a red dragon and had practiced it as well, and that had taken a weight off my mind. It had hurt Flick to find we'd kept a secret, but he'd understood why we hadn't said anything at first, and he'd been generally encouraging.

We'd tried to teach him after that, but we didn't have decent conditions and it wasn't going to get easier.

After that, we talked until we fell asleep. Neither of them had been awkward about waking up with us all on the same large bed, and I had bigger things to worry about today.

Like telling the whole world that dragons did exist and that I was their queen.

My stomach felt so tight I was afraid I was going to throw up, but I hadn't eaten anything for my stomach to give back to me. The rest of me was shaking, terrified of what they all might do.

I'd failed them all by letting out a demon intent on enslaving or killing everyone on the planet. I hadn't been directly responsible, but I had failed to power up his gate in time to stop him from breaking out of his prison.

"It's almost time," a woman said to me and then hurried away again.

I was grateful for the warning, but I wasn't entirely sure what was coming. Not without some kind of explanation.

It was clear I wouldn't be getting one when the people on the stage started talking.

A woman sat on a bright orange chair. Several more sat opposite and around the area. She seemed to be in charge and only let the others speak when she decided they could. If there was any pattern to it, I couldn't work it out.

They discussed what was happening and why, and the revelation that there were dragons, for several minutes before the woman cut through all the noise and chatter and brought everyone back to her. "It has been a day of many changes so far, and we've all learned a lot, but what can help us most at this point is speaking to a dragon themselves."

Silence followed this, and I was sure that I wanted to puke. Somehow, I held it together as she motioned for another chair to be put out and someone else motioned for me to walk onto the stage.

"Scarlet, a young woman from LA and also Queen of Detaris, the great dragon city, and the entire dragon population, please come in and have a seat."

"Thank you," I replied, trying to test my voice and make sure it worked. The words came out okay, but my voice was a little shaky.

I sank into the chair. Cameras flashed and the light sent bright spots into my eyes, making it harder to see.

"There are a lot of questions that any of us could ask you about where you are in life and what is going on. Many of them involve the dragon city you live in and how you've been able to go about your business and fight demons all the time." My host smiled as if she'd said something very normal, but I knew it wouldn't be anywhere near normal for pretty much everyone watching.

"There's a lot in that statement alone," I replied. "I haven't been queen for very long, and I've lived as a human and in the human community for most of my life."

"You don't look like much of a dragon right now. Can you explain how you are a dragon? Many don't believe it.

They think that maybe you *have* a dragon, or that the dragon is nothing but an illusion. That all the videos are fake. Can you shed some light on how you're sitting in front of us like a human but you are a dragon?"

I tilted my head to one side as I thought, trying to work out how to explain this or prove it in some way, then I remembered one of the first things I had done to get better control of my dragon transformation: changing a small subsection of the body at once.

I stretched out my hand and indicated that the cameras should all focus on it, then concentrated and shifted the skin from the pink fleshy softness of a human hand and arm to a more dragon-like appendage. My fingers became claws, and deep red scales spread.

There were gasps from those closest to me and some people shuffled further back.

"Go on, touch it and see for yourself," I said. "Hopefully it will help show you that dragons are real."

The presenter hesitated, but the guy next to her, who had been hanging back until now, was less scared and got up so he could come closer. He ran his hand slowly down my scales, his eyes going wide as he did.

"Wow. It's definitely very real, and this is your arm." He moved back, impressed.

His bravery helped to encourage others to give it a try and feel my scales. All of them sat back, satisfied that I wasn't entirely human.

"Thank you, everyone," the presenter said. "We have checked, stroked, and confirmed for ourselves that Scarlet here is a dragon with scales and the ability to shift between human and dragon form."

As she said the last few words, I went fully back to my human form. Although some dragons in Detaris had gotten used to holding a sort of halfway shift and appearing with patches of human features and skin and others of scales and dragon assets, I preferred to be one or the other entirely.

"Okay, so you are a dragon and you are a queen. You seem to do a lot of fighting, for a queen."

"I do. There is a threat that likes to plague my life and the lives of others. I first discovered it when a good friend of mine went missing and these *creatures* were looking for him and sniffing around. Eventually, they locked onto me and started chasing me. Sorry, mayor of LA. That park that looked like a train wreck had hit it and then somehow miraculously disappeared? I was learning to fly and running scared from one of my first ever shadow catcher encounters." I wasn't really that sorry for it. It wasn't as if I had done it deliberately, and I had done everything I could to get away from the demons another way.

It made the audience laugh, however, and it took the edge off the conversation we were having. Making them laugh was also something I hoped would endear them to me.

"And you have been fighting the same creatures ever since. Is that correct?"

I nodded. "They keep coming. Because I'm one of the few dragons left with the gift needed to harm them, they actively hunt my kind. But they will also hurt others nearby if someone gets too close and the drone-like demons don't have the more sensible mind of a handler to control them."

"But this hasn't been working lately?"

Thankful for the reporter's question, I seized my moment to talk to everyone about what had happened and how we were going to fix it.

I talked about how the gate had grown weaker but the knowledge to repair it had disappeared with time, and dragons who had been hunted down to almost nothing had taken the rest of the knowledge about it with them. Although I talked instead of answering the exact question, no one interrupted me as I explained what it had been like.

Despite telling my own story in my own words, there were things I left out. I didn't mention the bullies or Grigick, and I glossed over the majority of the difficulties I had been having with the elders.

By the time I was getting to the fateful journey to the gate and everything that had happened, I was sure that I was losing a few people, but thankfully, the news had captured a lot of that day.

"Most of you know what happened next. You've seen the footage, so I won't bore you with the details, other than to say, we did our best that day. Tried to get everything coordinated and information to the people who needed it. But humanity wasn't ready for this, and dragons have slowly made themselves less so."

"And the gate opened, exploding out another dragon?" The presenter asked the question with a lot of concern in her voice, but it was an awkward question and asked in such a way that I wasn't going to look good, no matter the answer.

"Firstly, I want to clarify that it was *not* a dragon. It may have looked like a dragon, but it isn't one. There are theories that once upon a time it might have been, but many, many lives ago. It is stretched thin now and much more like the demons it controls. Handlers are also similar. They were once creatures that have been corrupted and morphed and become part of something akin to shadow catcher and also partly a corrupted version of whatever they started as."

The presenter and other people nodded and asked some questions about the handler and main demon. I couldn't answer all of them, but I tried to do so to the best of my ability.

"Is there anything else you'd like to say before we open this up to questions from our audience and news reporters?" the presenter asked.

"Yes. That I'm sorry. It was my duty as queen and leader of the magical creatures of this world to protect you all. I failed. The demon has escaped its prison and now there is no telling exactly what it will do. I'm truly sorry. I will do everything I can to defeat it again and protect you all, as it is my duty to do."

There were a few murmurs at this, and I got the feeling it would create a few questions. Alitas had tried to prepare me for this earlier that morning. He'd been asking me difficult questions, and I had tried to be truthful while also being guarded.

After a little while, he had nodded and told me that I stood as good a chance as any at getting out of this one alive. Now I would see how much that preparation helped.

"It sounds as if you've screwed up a lot along the way. What makes you think you're fit to be queen?" The guy who'd said it was glaring at me. I wondered if there was any way to answer this question or if the guy simply wanted me to fail.

"It's easy to look at what's gone wrong in hindsight and make second guesses about what would have happened and who might be to blame, but no matter how much people want to act like they know better, the truth is, we all did our best at the time and could have done no more."

"So you're just ruling over us whether we want it or not?"

"I'm not ruling over anyone forcefully. I do not want to start civil wars, or any other kind of war. All I want to do is use my magic to pull the demon back and put him back in his eternal hell hole."

The questions continued, and despite my reassurances that they were safe and that I wouldn't rule over anyone, dragon or human, in a way they weren't okay with, some people couldn't grasp the logic and seemed to constantly be hitting a mental block. They wanted to charge me with a crime and declare me an illegitimate queen.

It got more and more out of control until one of the army soldiers stood up near the back of the tent and yelled at the top of his voice, "Enough! This is still the United States of America, and you are still all free citizens."

As he finished speaking, the crowd quieted and enough of them shuffled and sat that I was able to see to the back. It was Colonel Flint, and he gave me a grim smile and a curt nod before also sitting back down.

I appreciated the support from him all the more for how chaotic and angry it had begun to get. They weren't thinking clearly, and I didn't know how to calm them down properly.

"Why don't we take a short break?" the presenter said. "Scarlet can come back in a few minutes, and we'll talk more about the future and you can ask more questions about the role she plays and what is going on."

Relieved, I was soon up and on my feet and heading for an exit. It felt a little shameful to not stick around and to be clearly eager to leave, but I wasn't going to burst anyone's anger or happy bubble.

All I wanted was to find the demon king and get him back in his prison.

CHAPTER TWO

Once I was out of the hostile environment and the adrenaline had started to run out, I cried. Neritas and Alitas tried to comfort me, but I felt like a total failure. The demon had got out because of me.

"I've said this before, and I seem to need to say this again. You are not to blame." Alitas put a hand on my shoulder. "Everyone out there may be freaking out, but they'll get over it and get used to having a queen around on US soil *and* a president."

"I don't want anything from them. I'm not trying to make their lives harder. Just defeat a demon."

"And that is what will come out eventually. A sort of thank you for making life work despite all the danger and difficulties."

I nodded as the stagehand asked me if I was ready to go live again. I wasn't sure that I was, but they needed someone to talk to them and it was better me than anyone else.

More people had crammed their way into the tent.

Reporters from foreign delegations had joined as well, and more police. The latter was probably to help keep law and order among the humans.

With my head held high and a brief respite to take care of my mental state, I walked back on stage and retook my seat. Not quite everyone was ready, so I waited for a few seconds and looked around. After a while, I met the eyes of a young woman. She was standing in the reporter section, but I hadn't seen her in the previous round.

She smiled at me and waved. I returned the gesture, and she took a few steps forward, coming closer so that she might say something over the din of the crowd.

A cop came out to stop her from getting too close, but I waved my hand so they would let her through.

"I just wanted to say that I reported on your first public fight, around that restaurant, and I pored over that footage so many times. You risked your life to protect everyone around you and worked with the cops too. All because you decided it was for the best. Thank you. Thank you for saving lives when you could so easily have done anything else."

"You're welcome. I will always do my best."

"Was that a handler you killed at the end? He looked… almost human. As if he might once have been."

"He actually had once been a dragon, but preferred human form. He showed me his scales once, and I should have caught on then. They were a deeper black and different, like the demon's."

"Some of the dragons you flew with in the most recent attack were also black, though, weren't they?"

I nodded as I noticed that most of the rest of the room

had sat and were listening, while others were still finding their seats. This young woman had started the meeting back up again with her questions.

"Several very wonderful dragons I know are also black. A lot of the city guards are, the honor guard and many others. The color is different, but the difference is subtle." For the second time that day, I considered telling them that I could feel evil and good and I could tell them apart, and that I knew if someone meant harm and was controlled by the demon, or if they were safe.

Over the next twenty minutes, I answered some gentler questions, encouraging people to think for themselves and reiterating that we would do everything we could to protect people when the time came.

It didn't satisfy all of them, but some looked like they had begun to understand. Eventually, the politicians seemed to be fed up with talking in circles, and one of the more recognizable governors from a nearby state stood and waved for everyone to leave.

"Please stay in your seat," the nearest soldier said to me. "The US government would like to talk to you further. It might be useful for you to bring in your usual political advisers."

I nodded and suggested that Neritas, Flick, Alitas, Ben, Reijo, and Griffin were the dragons to choose for that.

Within seconds, we had enough chairs, and the presenters and her panels were leaving, taking their judgment with them. I didn't miss them, even knowing that they were just trying to care for their planet.

Faced with the US government, I felt out of my depth and wanted to run away with the humans who were leaving. I almost did. Did I have to do this? Would it really help? Or was I about to be arrested for breaking an insane number of laws? I had no way to know, but to wait. And I'd never much liked waiting.

The dragons I was familiar with most joined me soon enough that I didn't get too anxious about what might follow. As always, I had surrounded myself with dragons that formed a complete set of colors.

"Well done," Ben said when he was close enough to say it quietly so only I would hear.

I smiled, grateful for the vote of confidence. I was doing my best and had no idea what to expect.

Next, some of the people who had been near the top of the tent along with me came in closer. One of them, a man dressed in gray slacks and a pale blue polo shirt, walked straight up to me.

"I'm Senator Nichols. You seem to be an impressive young lady with a large burden on your shoulders."

I shrugged, not sure how to respond to that. I was who I was. "Apparently, this is what I was born to."

"I've never thought that power should be hereditary," a woman replied as she joined us.

"Power is never something I wanted, and if I hadn't proven worthy, I'd never have had it. The dragon community also cares that their leader does the right thing. And much like the US system works, there are others who are appointed by the people to keep the leader focused on doing their duty to their citizens. I would quickly lose my power if I didn't care enough."

"So the whole thing is a democracy too?" Senator Nichols asked.

"It's close enough," Ben replied for me. "There are dragons who are voted for, and they are helped by the royal line to care for the day-to-day, but the royal gets the final say on many things. While they hold a lot of power, they leave the governing to the voted-for representatives of each of our settlements."

"That sounds as if it could be abused." The first woman folded her arms across her chest, looking even more severe. I got the impression that no matter what any of us said, she would be trying to undermine my system and criticize it right now. It was hard not to feel defensive and insecure, but I fought the urge.

Several more people joined us, and I recognized some prominent politicians from other countries. I noticed an elderly man from the UK and seized onto the common ground.

"Think of it like the British monarchy," I suggested. "I may be queen and have the power and final say over many things, but just as the UK is recognized to be a democracy because the people have agency of their own and representatives they choose, so is the dragon world."

While the woman who had brought it up didn't seem to be much happier about my answer, this parallel mollified everyone else.

Senator Nichols helped to change the topic. "We understand that you also lead your army in a very practical way."

"Yes. I have abilities that mean I can combine the magical energy of other dragons into something more potent against the creatures we face."

"Which is the fighting we've seen? The very destructive fighting?"

"Is there any other kind of fight you can have against an enemy that decays everything it touches and is relentless in its destruction or enslavement of all living things?" I didn't appreciate the tone of the comment and struggled to keep my temper from heading out of control. I wasn't here to be made to feel like a villain.

"This enemy is as new to us as dragons are." Senator Nichols' voice was still calm. "Understanding you would help us understand them, I think."

The military officials present all echoed this, so I spent the next hour detailing everything I could about the enemy we shared. Not long into it, the rest of the government officials all came back, as well as everyone else who was considered to have the clearance to listen to this part of the conversation.

Once they were all there, I started again, recapping the information and already tired of the politics.

Trying to be thorough, I described the enemy and what fighting them was like. Ben and Alitas helped me. They both had studied the footage that the human world already had of me fighting them and what the shadow catchers and their handlers were capable of.

I was grilled on them, despite giving what information I could.

"So in reality, you barely know more than we can figure out from these videos ourselves," one of the generals said. He was an older man with an extra chin and so many medals pinned to one side of his chest that I wondered if he looked like a pin cushion underneath.

"I know everything the dragons are sure of and we're

looking through our archives for more as we can. If I learn any more, I will share it. But this demon has been trapped for millennia, and the records from when he was last at large are few. From my understanding, as the gate has weakened, the presence of the other, lesser, demons has grown. Until very recently, no one needed to know about them because we all thought the threat was a thing of the past."

I didn't say anything. I had repeated myself enough.

"There is one question that no one has asked yet, that I would very much like the answer to. I think a lot of how we proceed depends upon it." The senator sat forward, making it clear he was listening intently.

"What would that be?" I asked when he paused for too long for my liking.

"Why did the gate weaken in the first place? You have said that you were trying to strengthen it. To power it with the...magic that you all possess. Why wasn't this done sooner?"

I paused before answering this question. Alitas had warned me that it would be asked and that they weren't likely to respond well to my answer. It wasn't an easy question to answer. I didn't know all the details, and neither did any of us. Alitas had never been privy to all the information in the heads of the red dragons he had served, and neither had his predecessor.

"It's complicated, but it comes down to several varied reasons. Most recently, that no one was left alive who could do anything about it. My powers are rare among my kind, and it was a secret that we held that kind of power. Partially so it wouldn't be abused, and partially so it wouldn't be held in too high a regard." The last part I added, hoping it was as true as I made it sound.

Some people around me nodded along, but I could see others growing more restless. If they didn't like this part of my answer, they weren't going to like what I followed it with. I had nothing good to add.

"The other reasons stem from the dragons' past. My father was one of only a few who had any ability to power the gate, and he was hunted by others of our kind who didn't understand the importance our line played in protecting the gate. As were his relatives. The other big reason is that at some point in our past, one of the mad monarchs opted to erase mention of the gate and what it did from our history, as well as everything my kind of dragon was capable of. No one knows why and we have no one to ask."

My words created a stir, and everyone talked among themselves for a while. I looked at Ben and Alitas. I couldn't change the past and I wasn't responsible for it, but I got the feeling that I was going to be blamed and held accountable for everything anyway.

"What are you going to do about the gate?" Senator Nichols was gentle with the question but voiced what everyone else was thinking.

"I have no idea. This should never have happened. I was in the middle of trying to fix it when your soldiers shot the gate up and finished breaking it. Since then, I am as in the dark as all of you."

"Are you blaming the US military for this?" one of the generals demanded.

"No. I'm not blaming anyone. I just know I was doing

what I could. As I've always done." I shrugged. A part of me wanted to say yes. That the US military had frelled up my mission and possibly screwed the entire world over. I swallowed those words and left it there, however.

"Thank you, Scarlet," the senator said. "I think we have talked over all we can process for one day. I know that there are likely to be more questions, but for now, let us adjourn and come back when we can talk more."

I wasn't going to argue about ending the meeting. It had grown uncomfortable, and as much as I thought the viewers would be more sympathetic, especially those from other countries, I was done with trying to be politically correct and tactful for a while. Fighting shadow catchers was easier. I just had to kill them or be killed.

This room was full of people who were so guarded and had so many different agendas that I had no idea who was friend or foe, let alone how to fight any enemies. It was exhausting.

CHAPTER THREE

Ben and Alitas were at my side, followed by Neritas and Flick a fraction of a second later. They smiled at me and escorted me outside and back to Detaris without letting anyone else talk to me.

We had taken a few steps beyond the edge of the tent and toward Detaris again when I heard a familiar voice calling my name.

I turned toward a small group of women to see Stephanie, Alice, and several others of my friends. Alice looked as if she was still cross that I hadn't shown up for work one day, but Stephanie beamed at me.

Putting up a hand, I let my bodyguards know I wanted to stop and talk to them. Stephanie gave me less than a second before she pulled me into a hug and held on tightly.

"You worried us half to death." Stephanie finally let me go and Alice frowned at me. For a second, I wondered if I was about to get fired officially.

"So you left the shop and café to go be a queen?" Alice asked.

"Something like that," I replied. "It's a little more complicated."

"Several other dragons tried to kill her first," Neritas added, grinning at the women who were suddenly very interested in my companions.

"We kept her safe. Flew with her and defended her when the other dragons tried to attack. Made sure most never tried it again." Flick came in beside him, wanting some attention too.

I rolled my eyes. Trust my two original bodyguards to want the attention the second a female appeared. They were such flirts.

"I have so much to tell you all now that I don't have to keep it a secret, but I don't know if I can do it right now." I instantly felt a pang of regret. These people had been my whole life, besides Anthony. I wanted to talk to them and find out how they were all doing and tell them everything.

Before I could pull away, Brenta approached me. The elders had waited nearby for the meetings just in case. I wondered if I was about to get told off in a whole new way. Being openly a dragon was still very new, but I didn't see why I couldn't talk to my friends now that they knew.

"Would you all like to visit Detaris and stay with us for a few days to catch up with Scarlet?" Brenta asked.

I fought not to show my shock at her offer as my friends eagerly accepted it. They would be the first humans to stay in the great dragon city. I immediately thought of how many steps it meant they were going to have to climb. It probably wasn't something the rest of the dragon population thought much of. Most of them could fly from a young age, and kids weren't expected to go to the top of the tallest tower at the far back of the city anyway.

With my friends in tow, we returned to the city. It was fun to see the awe on their faces as they crossed the threshold and saw the entire city for the first time. I'd been living in it for over a year and the beauty of it was still not something I was used to.

We paused there as I let them watch dragons flying around and the guards noticed we were back. A lot of the more senior members had come with me and the elders, but they hung back as well, bringing up the rear.

My mother had stayed in the city. We'd all wanted a red dragon to be safe during whatever happened, a failsafe until we were sure that we weren't going to be betrayed and taken prisoner. Not that I thought anyone could kill me very easily, but this way, if I died, my mother could lead in my stead.

She came to me first, and the relief was clear on her face. "I watched the whole thing. Well done, Scarlet. You handled a difficult situation well."

"I could have handled it better." I exhaled. I was grateful for the support, but I didn't think I'd done as well as she thought.

She hugged me. "I'm glad you're back safe."

As she pulled back I motioned to my friends and introduced them one by one. "This is my mom, Sienna."

"Your mom?" Stephanie almost squealed the question.

I nodded. I had a lot to tell everyone, and I barely knew where to begin.

After a few more introductions where I formally introduced Neritas, Flick, and Ben, we made our way deeper into the city. While there was a path to follow, most of the dragons left us alone, but as in the past, lots of them landed once we reached the official gateway to the city.

The elders gathered around to talk to my friends and ex-boss. Griffin joined Brenta to shake their hands.

"Thank you for being here for Scarlet. It is wonderful for us to begin our relationship with the human race by inviting in the friends of our own queen. She has spoken highly of you in the past," Griffin said, although I couldn't remember ever mentioning them. It was finally obvious why Brenta had invited them in, however.

My friends were people who were inclined to like us already. They liked me and knew I wasn't scary. It was a soft launch to people who were warmed up by association.

"Scarlet never breathed a word about not being human," Alice replied. "Not one of us had a clue."

"That's 'cause I didn't know either." I shrugged as I motioned for everyone to go forward and for the elders to take the lead. This was their idea and I wanted to hang back and catch up with my friends while they were shown the city.

They weren't led too high, to begin with. We went to one of the larger towers with a restaurant, taking wide bridges and smooth paths. It had grown late while I had been talking and it wasn't long until lunchtime, so we stopped there and almost entirely took over the restaurant.

It wasn't my favorite one in the city, but it was still good, and I was able to sit with my friends for the first time and talk to them properly.

"Can you really turn into a dragon as well and fly?" Stephanie asked.

I nodded, unable to keep from smirking. In a lot of ways, it was a dream come true to be able to fly. "When we're outside again, I'll show you."

"Is it possible to carry other people?"

Although I hadn't tried, I didn't see why not. Once, the flying teacher, Jared, had carried a bunch of us into battle, all of us riding on his back as humans. It took me a few minutes to find the video, and I had to get help from Ben to search for it, but eventually we showed them the video of the fight.

Because the handlers had been out of the city limits and the cloak that hid it from view, Jared had burst through it in dragon form with six of us riding on his back. It looked even more epic than I'd imagined to see him transform into his human form, the white dragon disappearing and dropping us all to the ground.

We'd landed hard but got into the fight right away. We'd tried some of the new equipment we'd got from the caves near the gate, including the flying disks, and the shadow catchers quickly died.

It was the first time we had been up against multiple handlers, and it reminded me how many of us it had taken to make any progress. We'd come a long way since then.

I'd only planned to show them the flying part, but everyone gathered around to watch us win and go back into the city's cloak again. The human who had taken it on his phone continued to film from his hiding place among the trees on the opposite side of the road. I cut it there, however.

"That is probably the coolest video I've seen of you," Stephanie said. "That's so badass. I can hardly believe it's you, but I'm glad I encouraged you to go looking for your friend. I thought it was just going to be some Mexican drug cartel or something. Not actual real-life dragons."

"I wondered if it was going to be some kind of dragon cult. They had these necklaces." I stopped speaking, realizing that no one had ever explained what they were. What had the necklaces meant? I knew that Anthony's had glowed briefly and he had left it behind. Ben had let me keep it, but I couldn't remember where I had put it.

This wasn't the time to ask him. The elders encouraged the group to continue onward. I had no idea where this tour was meant to be ending up, but we were soon outside, winding up and taking bridges as the elders led my friends around the city. I took this opportunity to turn into a red dragon for a while to relieve my aching legs.

It felt good to fly, something I never got to do enough. Now, hopefully, that would change. If the humans knew about us, perhaps I would be able to fly outside the city. It would feel strange at first, but I was hopeful.

Flying around impressed my friends and gave me the much-needed opportunity to spread my wings. It felt amazing to be able to fly again, and I took a moment to enjoy it before coming back toward my friends and hovering near them.

Brenta smiled at my friends while I hovered nearby. "This would actually be a good opportunity to cut out long flights of stairs on the way to our next destination."

Flick grinned as he fell backward off the edge of a bridge. He let himself fall for half a second before transforming into his dragon form. They gasped and rushed forward to check if he was all right, but he swiftly recovered and flew up.

With two of us in dragon form, we had enough space for my friends to climb onto our backs and hold on. We took three each. It was strange to be in dragon form carrying humans, but I liked how in awe they were. I'd hidden being a dragon for so long that it had never occurred to me that being in dragon form around humans might be fun.

With the humans all holding on tight, we lifted from the tower and flew higher. Alitas and the elders all leaped off the bridge and transformed as well, and Brenta took the lead as Alitas, Ben, and Neritas came around and over me, protecting me from any possible danger.

No one in the city had been threatening toward me for several weeks now. The threat from the demon and the elders' full support of me stopped any animosity from before. Being crowned as their queen helped as well. Any attack on me would now be punished a lot more severely, and everyone knew it.

I flew carefully and smoothly, noticing Flick doing the same, not showing off while he carried the precious burden of my friends. My dragon form was so strong that I could barely feel their weight on my back. They were tiny in comparison to me.

Brenta flew us up and to the back of the city, cutting out a significant portion of the climb my friends would have needed to attempt. She entered the edge of the elders' chambers and turned back into a human again. I slowed as I came close, and I stayed in dragon form and paused as close to the edge as I could get.

It wasn't easy staying perfectly steady, but Neritas took human form again and helped my friends down from my back. I then took human form and helped the rest off Flick.

By the time everyone was in human form and standing in the elders' chambers, Brenta and Griffin had given orders for more chairs and tables to be arranged, and had snacks and drinks brought to us. I joined my friends around one of the tables and relaxed for the first time in days.

Somewhere, a demon was on the loose, but for at least another hour or two, I was going to put it behind me and focus on catching up with my friends and telling them about my new life. They had a lot of questions about how everything worked. Ben helped me answer some of the more complicated ones.

Brenta joined us as well, although she didn't say much, just listened in and added answers if she could to a question.

I relaxed, feeling a strange contentment at finally bringing two parts of my life together. My mother soon joined us again as well, and I had the opportunity to give her a further glimpse into my human life.

Eventually, our lunch forgotten, we ate the food and various drinks, and then I offered to take my friends to the royal tower to hang out for a while. I couldn't leave it much longer before I refocused on work and the aftermath of the interviews I'd done, but I didn't want to miss out on spending time with them whenever I was free.

Now, however, I had a demon to find and figure out how to trap it again. If it was even still possible.

CHAPTER FOUR

Waking up in the royal tower was always something I loved, but it was extra special to wake up to the sound of familiar voices and hear my friends from both parts of my life talking to each other over breakfast.

I often left the room door slightly open so I could hear if trouble arose, and today was no different. Except it wasn't trouble I heard, but the wonderful sound of people I cared about.

Excited and grateful that the rest of the previous day had gone without a hitch, I got up and hurried out to them.

"Good morning, Scarlet," Ben said. "We were just introducing your friends to the delight of breakfast as a queen."

I grinned as I looked at the breakfast table and all the food it was laden with. He had a point. If it had been for me alone, it would have been an insane amount. As it was, it was too much for all of us anyway.

"The human world looks to be taking your interview well," Reijo said as he appeared with his cell phone in his hand. He had a news channel on it and he sat down, barely looking up long enough to be polite.

"They believe it?" I asked. I'd assumed that many of them would still think it was fake.

"I guess when you have leaders of different countries all meeting with you and talking about it as if it's true, the rest of the world has to concede it's true as well." Reijo shrugged as if he didn't quite understand how so many had shifted from not believing we were real to believing it so fast.

I sat and piled a plate high with food and made idle small talk with my friends while everyone else slowly woke up and joined us.

"Do you think you'll spend your life visiting important people and defending the world now?" Stephanie asked me when I'd finished eating.

"Hopefully not. I want to get this demon back where he ought to be before he hurts anyone, if we can, and then I want to focus on making sure the dragons are okay. So many of my predecessors neglected their needs. And now that the world knows about us, I should be able to fix a lot of issues."

Alice put a hand on my shoulder. "I'm proud of you. I know I gave you a hard time when you didn't come back to work. If I'd known what you were facing and the responsibility you were going to have to bear, I'd have been far gentler and more supportive."

I smiled and felt tears sting the backs of my eyes. "You couldn't have known, but it helps to hear that now. I don't always know what to do and I have made a lot of mistakes. I'd have appreciated your wisdom."

Before she could share any of it with me now, Capricia flew in, transforming as she did. "The demon. He's attacking a human settlement. It's on the news, and the humans are trying to get our attention."

"Crap. That was fast. Where?" I asked, shaking.

Reijo quickly pulled up the news feed Capricia instructed him to. "Somewhere called Denver."

"That's miles and miles away. What does he want in Denver?"

No one answered me as we all crowded around to see the small phone screen and gauge the damage.

The large, red, demonic dragon was soaring above a couple of buildings in the city. Down on the ground was the usual array of shadow catchers, and I quickly spotted a handler as well. But scarier were the birds and other creatures that were rushing around and attacking any humans that got in their way.

"How long ago was this?" I watched a woman defending the doorway to a building being attacked repeatedly by birds and creatures before the shadow catchers reached her.

"Ten minutes. Maybe more," Capricia replied.

"We need to get there and help them." I rushed to grab my pack, sword, and shield.

"We aren't going to make it in time," Ben called out to me. I swore as I strapped everything on me anyway and reached out with my mind to charge everything.

If this demon was going to attack people, I had to show the human race that he wasn't one of us and that I was going to try to protect them from him.

"Fly," Capricia said. "We all can."

After a fraction of a second of stunned silence, every dragon in the room started moving and getting ready to leave. Multiple conversations started up at once as Alitas put Neritas and Flick in charge of protecting me while he went to get as many honor guards as he could and Capricia flew off to get city guards.

Griffin flew in, his face white, as I went over to my human friends.

"Stay here if you all can. You'll be safe, and I'm sure the elders will see that you're looked after until we get back."

Stephanie caught my arm. "Can we help?"

"Probably not. Not this time." I frowned, not wanting to put her in harm's way, but trying to think quickly of how she could help. Without weapons I could charge, they would be in my way more than a help. And there were a lot of unknowns with this battle.

With my armor stowed in another bag and my shield strapped to my back, I went over to my mother.

"You should stay here too, just in case," I told her, grateful that I could leave the city in her hands.

"If I didn't know that Neritas and Flick have your back and can help you in similar ways, I wouldn't be able to stay," she whispered back. I grinned, wishing she could come with me. She was one of a few who knew that Neritas and Flick were both learning to use the red dragon powers.

Neritas had shown himself to be almost as adept as me, and Alitas had also begun training himself and Flick. Flick had a harder time grasping it at first, but he soon begun to take hold of magic, combine it, and make it work for the group.

The biggest problem we were going to have was the lack of red dragons in general. While our basic power was relatively obsolete in the human world, it combined with the magic of other colored dragons to create an effect that killed the demonic forces trying to rule Earth. Without the red magic as well, we were fairly sure that they could still be hurt and killed, but we hadn't put that to the test yet.

"Okay, everyone ready to leave?" I asked. My royal tower was suddenly full of dragons.

There were nods as I looked around the group. It wasn't as large as the set of dragons I had tried to power the gate with, but we had no time to gather the rest.

I launched myself out of the door, transforming as I did and taking to the skies. More dragons came in around the group as I did, and for a moment I panicked.

In the past, I had been attacked enough times that now I expected the worst. When no violence came and the dragons simply joined the formation and flew with me, I relaxed again. I headed east and a little north, hoping that someone else knew how to fly to Denver. I knew the rough direction, but I had never flown this far before.

We burst through the city shield and out into the open to shouts and calls from the humans nearby. Despite the story now being out and the city no longer a secret, there were plenty of people camping outside to get a glimpse of us.

Cameras flashed as over half of them pulled out their phones and took photos and video footage. It was strange to think of so many of them wanting to see us.

Despite them calling and trying to wave us down, I didn't slow or give them any obvious signs of attention.

Denver was my only thought, and my desire to get there as fast as possible.

Does anyone know the way? I asked the entire dragon group.

I do. Alitas shifted slightly, putting on a small burst of speed until he was out in front of me, but still in his usual protective spot above me.

Not long after he moved, Kryos also shifted, above as well but now right behind Alitas and protecting the gap that the captain of my honor guard had created. I appreciated their care, although I didn't know what sort of threat we would find out here. Until we got close to the demon, we were masters of the skies.

I tried not to think about how much destruction he could cause in the time it was taking us to get there, and I encouraged Alitas to fly as fast as he could.

I'll guard from the rear and make sure we don't lose anyone, Jared told me and the lead group. His voice was a welcome addition. He was one of the dragons who had joined us when he'd seen us all flying out.

It was strange to have so many dragons with us as we flew, but we still missed Jace and everyone who was usually with her. They'd gone back to the farmhouse the previous evening to get supplies, having never intended to stay with us for long. If we'd had them this would have been the largest force we'd ever flown with.

We'd been flying for half an hour when a large group of dragons appeared on the horizon to the north, matching our trajectory and slowly easing in closer. I recognized Jace and Cios almost immediately. The pair was leading a group of about fifteen more dragons.

Good to see you, I thought only to her.

Didn't think I'd let you have all the fun, did you, Red?

I grinned and let out a small roar of delight. Despite the fear I felt for the humans ahead of us, it was good to be flying.

More humans noticed us, especially when we flew over larger settlements. Some shouted, many pointed and called to others, and yet more of them reached for phones to record our passing in some way.

I didn't doubt that they would have worked out where we were heading already, and that social media would have been abuzz with our flight. All I could hope was that the military saw us as an aid on our way to defend everyone.

Almost as if they had read my mind as well, a squadron of fighter jets came up alongside us from our south. I had no way of talking to them in my dragon form, but I kept a respectful distance from them and tried not to look aggressive. Jace was close enough now that she tucked her group in with mine as we raced toward Denver.

The ground below us sped by as I pushed everyone with me to fly hard. None of us were used to this—not even the city guards spent long periods in the air—but we all knew what was at stake.

After a couple of hours, the group slowed and the fighter jets started to get ahead of us.

I think the back of this group needs to rest, even if just for ten minutes, Jared said. The serious tone of his voice was enough to let me know that he was concerned.

Okay. Let's land somewhere out of the way and take a break, eat and drink, and then get back in the air. Maybe we can get more intel while we're down on the ground.

I led the downward trajectory as I spotted the edge of some farmland and a couple of large fields that had been left for cattle grazing and were currently empty. Whoever owned it, I could only hope they didn't mind us landing there. As I descended, I noticed the jets responding to our landing as they circled to keep an eye on us. There was a road to one side, a tarmac for them to land on if they needed to, but I could understand their reluctance for now.

Right before I touched down, I transformed back into my human form, realizing as my feet hit solid ground that I was exhausted.

It wasn't easy to fly so far, but I hoped we had made good progress. Everyone else followed suit, taking human form as they landed. Not everyone managed it as smoothly, especially the dragons who had slipped to the back of the group. They were clearly worn out, and it made me wonder if I could use magic to strengthen them as I had with us in human form in the past.

My first thoughts were still to find out what was going on, and I pulled out my phone at the same time Ben did, searching for the latest news. There were a lot of edited videos of the earliest part of the attack that were still being shown, and then it progressed. The demon was targeting two specific side-by-side buildings.

One was a large, modern church building of some kind, and the other was a business that happened to be beside it. I didn't know the significance of either, or of any logic behind the attack, but the military had turned up and formed barriers around the buildings before the shadow catchers had reached them.

The defense was weak and people were still getting

hurt, but it was slowing the advance down. With any luck, it would keep many of the civilians alive until we could get there.

I wished I could get in the air again immediately after watching, but Neritas thrust a canteen of water into my hands and followed it with a cereal bar. As I started on the latter, I noticed the jets slowing and coming in to land on the road beside us.

"Clear some space just in case and come away from the road," I called to my whole group.

Used to my commands, especially in battle situations and away from the city, everyone hurried over to me despite how tired they were. It gave the jets room to land, although they had to time it very precisely and come in one by one before swinging out of the way.

When the first jet was stationary and the pilot had gone through their usual landing checks, they popped the top hatch and lifted themselves out. I went over toward them.

"I hope we didn't scare anyone," I said when I was close enough to talk.

"It was definitely a new sight, but you look like you're heading to Denver and, if so, you're more than welcome."

I nodded as another jet landed, making it impossible to talk until they switched off their engine.

Alitas, Ben, Neritas, and Flick had followed me over and we discussed what was going on briefly.

"Are you heading all the way there with us?" I asked once several more pilots had landed and joined us.

"Should be. They need help. Any way you can make us more effective at teaching this son of a bitch a lesson?" the head pilot asked.

"I was about to offer to." I grinned as I drew on the magic from all the dragons in the field and connected to the entire plane beside me. I supercharged it and anything inside that felt like ammunition as well.

I quickly moved to do the rest.

"That should be all of them." I shook hands with the pilots. They were all grateful. "I got the planes too, so if anything demonic comes at you, contact with the plane will hurt them, but it won't be enough to kill them without me recharging you and it won't protect you for long."

"We'll take whatever you can give us in this fight."

With everything I could do to help done and sorted, I took another swig of water from the canteen Neritas kept close by and returned to the dragons to figure out if I could get them back in the air again.

They needed us in Denver, and I didn't intend to keep them waiting any longer than necessary.

CHAPTER FIVE

It took far longer to get everyone back in the air than I had hoped for, and with each passing minute the jets and more tired dragons needed help, I grew more worried. I tried to use magic to help everyone, but I would need as much as possible for the coming battle.

Eventually, we were back in formation and flying hard toward Denver again. A few more dragons from nearby cities had joined us in the air to respond to the threat. It was support that made me glad, especially as I hadn't been able to visit every dragon city in the area yet.

Knowing that there were more dragons in more cities who were willing to come to our aid gave me confidence that I would be able to defend the people. I had beaten this demon every time we'd encountered him or his forces in the past.

The videos of the attacks that had happened so far replayed in my head, however. So much had been destroyed already and so many people had been harmed. I didn't understand all of the forces the demon was using, but I knew I had to stop him.

I grew more cautious as the smudge on the horizon came fully into view and I realized it was Denver. The attack had happened in the north of the city, so I adjusted my course slightly, moving to intercept him.

As I grew closer, I looked for the demon in the air and felt for the presence of his forces with my mind, but I couldn't pick up on anything by feel or visually. If the demon was nearby, he was somehow masking himself.

Despite that, I flew hard and fast, picking up speed, even if it meant that I left the weaker of my forces behind. I had been patient up until this point.

Fearing the worst, I scanned the city's skyline and looked for the buildings I had seen in the videos. It took me a few more seconds to find them. There was no sign of the deep red demon in dragon form. He was long gone.

Letting out an angry roar, I swooped down to get a better look at what had happened and to see if anyone was still in danger. There were still some shadow catchers down here. My mind was able to feel them here and there, but not in the numbers, the news had been showing.

The two buildings he'd attacked had been broken into and the barriers decayed to the point they looked like something from a post-apocalyptic movie. I was too late. We were too late.

I had barely been in the vicinity for more than half a minute when one of the humans nearby ran up and jumped. As they did, they transformed into a green dragon and flew toward me.

Scarlet? they asked, a young male voice sounding in my

head. He had an accent that placed him somewhere nearby, although I couldn't tell exactly where.

Yes. Did you come here to help defend these people? I asked, hoping they had succeeded though I knew they likely had not.

We tried. We failed. He was too strong. As soon as his handlers had whatever he came here for, the majority of them retreated. We focused on saving who we could and protecting as many innocent lives and bystanders from being caught up in the destruction as possible.

Thank you, I replied, wishing I could show this young dragon all the gratitude I truly felt. We hadn't gotten here in time, but at least some of our kind had shown up and done what they could.

My relief was short-lived. I approached the area my new friend flew toward, and I saw how many injured and dying there were. More had been hurt than I had anticipated. The human medics had set up a sheltered area with a pop-up awning and gathered many of their kind and mine underneath.

I turned back into human form as I landed and hurried to the nearest person who looked like they could be saved. I reached into a pocket and pulled out one of the healing devices that our magic could power.

I didn't wait for the dragons with me to land. I pulled on the magic in my shield, armor, and sword to power the device and heal the human in front of me. They had so many marks and rotted sections of their flesh where they had stood up to a shadow catcher or some other minion of the demon that it took some time to aid them.

I healed as many of them as I could, using a combination of magic and their body's natural resources, and their faces grew easier and their breathing less labored. By the time they appeared stable and the medical professionals nearby took over trying to make them comfortable, I had moved on.

More of my dragons landed and came over to me. Neritas and Flick still flanked me in case there was danger I hadn't foreseen. They quickly pulled out healing devices of their own.

The few of us who could use them moved among the crowds, healing humans and dragons, whoever appeared to need it most. It didn't feel like enough. So many people were wounded that yet another person always needed help.

"Find out what happened," I asked Ben when he looked lost and as if he didn't know how to help.

He nodded and hurried away. Two minutes later, the captain of the fighter jets strode in. I expected him to go to some kind of superior officer, or whoever was in charge of the medical operation, but he came over to me.

"We did a quick circle of the area before landing. No sign of the dragon anywhere."

"Demon," I replied swiftly enough and automatically enough that my irritation was clear. "He's not a dragon. Might have been once, but he's not anymore. Corrupted and a lot harder to kill."

"Comforting," he said as he frowned. "Do you know where he might have gone?"

I shook my head. Until two days earlier, he had been locked behind a gate. "I don't even know what he came here for and why he did this."

The pilot didn't reply but came to my side as I moved to

the next injured person and began the healing process. They shifted as I did, not lucid or actively recognizing what was going on.

He gently soothed them and encouraged them to relax while I healed the decayed flesh and bite marks down one side of their body. It took several minutes to make enough difference that they regained some composure and understanding of what was happening.

"Are you an angel?" she asked. Her voice was weak, but her focus was back and her breathing was calming.

"No. Just able to do a few things humans can't. But I'm no saint, and I'm human in lots of other ways." I smiled as the healing device reached the end of what it could do. She looked a lot better than she had, but she was still going to take some time to recover. From the haunted look on her face, I suspected the emotional toll would be far worse.

Before I went to another person, Ben returned. His jaw was set and he hurried to me in a manner that reminded me of Anthony when he had news someone wasn't going to like.

"What did the demon do?" I asked. Even if it was the worst news ever, I was Earth's first line of defense and that meant I had to know and try to combat whatever it was.

"He was looking for something. And his handlers seem to have found it, although no one appears to know exactly what it was."

I raised an eyebrow and shuffled around a table to reach yet another woman who needed healing.

As I healed her, Ben explained that it had started with the birds. All of them in the vicinity had started to attack the people in and around these two buildings. I listened, channeling magic and doing what little I could while he told me that the shadow catchers had come next, but by then, some people had started to defend themselves.

Guns had been pulled on the birds, but the people wielding them hadn't had the confidence that the military did, and while they had shot at the birds, there had been nothing regimented or skillful. Some birds were killed, showing that these creatures weren't like the shadow catchers and could be killed by human weapons.

Except they had done damage to the people here. Many of the wounded sported beak marks with the start of decay around them. It was almost as if these birds were half normal, albeit aggressive, and half shadow catcher.

I shuddered as I thought about it. No one had been ready for this, but we should have been. We'd been so busy having diplomatic meetings, and then I'd rested on my laurels with my human friends, wanting to impress them and show them my new life. But I'd wasted my time and not been prepared for this.

"Scarlet! I know what you're doing. Don't blame yourself for this," Neritas said as he came to my side again. He looked drained and tired, as if he'd used all the magic he had to heal people. And somehow, he had read my mind and known what I was doing.

"I have no one else to blame." I fed him a little magic to make him feel better, taking it almost exclusively from myself.

"There is no one human to blame for this. Or dragon. A demon came here to steal and destroy. All you can do is try to fight back and arm those who would do the same." Neritas tucked his healing device back in his pocket.

Looking around the tent, I saw hurting people we still hadn't gotten to, but we had pulled a lot of the magic out of our crew already. I was in danger of taking too much.

Despite that, I couldn't stand to see people hurting if something could be done. I went to the next and started healing them anyway, doing just enough to ease their pain and make sure they would recover in time. It wasn't entirely fair, compared to those I had already helped, but it was the best I could do. We'd never had to heal so many that we'd run short on resources.

Although he was tired, Neritas tried to copy me and heal as well, but he only managed a few more before I saw him pause and put a hand to his head. This time I took his healing device from him.

"Enough. Get some food and rest and give me a few minutes longer. I'm going to do what else I can and then I want to go see what the shadow catchers were aiming for and what it looks like." I dreaded seeing the attack site directly. I remembered what Reijo's house had looked like when we had gone looking for him and been ambushed by shadow catchers controlled by Fintar.

If I was to learn anything from this to help fight the demon, however, finding it myself was the only way.

There were still injured people when I ran out of the ability to heal more, and guilt almost brought me to my knees where the exhaustion I felt hadn't yet succeeded. Several of them were in pain but aware enough to reach out for me or look at me with understanding and hope.

I promised to come back as soon as my magic regenerated, and I walked away from the tent. Immediately, most of the dragons flocked to me. They had felt the magic drain from them and were feeling rough after flying so far so quickly.

"Rest, please. As well as you can under the circumstances. We need to figure out what happened here and then get back to Detaris."

"If you're going in there, then at least some of us are coming with you," Alitas replied, no doubt thinking of my safety. I knew better than to argue with the captain of the honor guard when it came to escorting me, but I ushered others away to recuperate until I was left with a familiar few dragons who often formed my company when I dared danger.

Lifting my head, both to look as if I was in charge and to help hide how exhausted I was, I strode toward the first of the two buildings. I was still several yards off the decayed side with a gaping hole in it when the captain of the fighter jets came up to me again.

"Mind if I join you in finding out what the hell happened here?" he asked.

"Not at all. Just be careful where you step and what you touch. I wouldn't want any residue they leave behind to hurt you or an errant demon to attack." I smiled and hoped that this soldier could take some direction from me. Some struggled with it.

Once more, I paused on the threshold. The inside of the building was dark and in bad shape. Decay and attacks from birds and shadow catchers had shattered glass, bent supports, and made floors weak. It was a death trap. But I still needed to go inside.

"None of you have to come in here with me," I added as

I thought back to being buried alive after a previous fight with the demons and fleeing down tunnels.

All of them stuck with me, determined to go wherever I did. Neritas, Flick, and Alitas all came closer, protective in all ways. I wanted to turn and run. The memory of all the soil on top of me and not knowing if I was going to get out made my heart race and my palms sweat.

Pushing the fear aside, I stepped forward and made myself shine enough to light the view before me. I had answers to find.

CHAPTER SIX

I was barely a hundred yards into the building when I saw the slimy, decayed trail of the shadow catchers. The church was a shadow of its former glory, and the entire inside would have to be ripped out, fixed, and put back together if it was ever going to be used again.

It seemed the shadow catchers hadn't been interested in anything that had any value to the humans who used it. None of the religious items or the money the church had last collected had been touched. All of it was off to one side while a trail led toward the middle of the building.

Thankfully, the thinner path and the lack of any resistance had led to the building remaining more stable deeper in, and the supporting pillars and walls were more intact. It made me feel a little bolder as I went deeper. If the building was going to collapse on us, it was at least less likely here.

The trail of decay and slime continued all the way to the back of the building where, with the power out and no windows, it got darker. Despite the drain on my magic, I made myself brighter to compensate. I wanted to figure this out.

As we went back and found what looked like a decayed set of stone steps going down under the floor, a guy shuffled in from a back door.

It was a man I had healed ten minutes earlier. He smiled as he saw me and hobbled along.

"The critters went down there. Didn't even know we had a room under there. Someone must have paved over it or blocked it off in some way."

"Did they come straight here?" I asked, pausing at the top of it and being careful what I touched. I held my hand up like a torch to look down, but it was the beginning of a long corridor and I couldn't see far from up here.

"They stopped if there was resistance from us, but they seemed to know what they were looking for. Eventually, we worked out that if we didn't get in their way and they didn't really notice us, they would leave us alone. But... everything they touched melted. All of it."

I put a hand on his shoulder, trying to provide a little comfort. He gave me a wan smile, but I could see he was still in pain, and more than physical. This building had meant something to him.

"I'm sorry this happened to you. They're not human and they're uncaring, but I am hoping to beat them and see the world safe."

He exhaled and looked around at the building that was in ruins around us.

"It won't save this church, but maybe it can ensure they don't take something like this from other people. Is there anything I can do to help?"

I shook my head instinctively. From what he'd said and his injuries, he'd already done more than enough for any human put in his situation.

"Go and rest. We'll figure this out from here."

"If you find anything, will you bring it up so we can see it?" he asked, leaning toward the hole to look down.

I doubted I would find anything, but I reassured him that I'd let him know what was down there and then opted to take the plunge.

"I'm going to walk down the sides where the decay is the least," I said to the others.

"Put your hands out on the walls too," Alitas said. "It can help you stay steady if a little crumbles and help us catch you if a lot goes."

I was surprised he was letting me go first if he thought it was that dangerous. He followed, however, coming second and keeping close to me.

I tried not to think about where we might be going as I planted a hand on each wall and walked down the steps with my legs more splayed than normal as I kept to the edges.

Thankfully the stairway was narrow, and it didn't require much of a straddle to miss the decayed middle section. It felt like not many shadow catchers had been down here, as if some of the ones we were following had stopped at the top, possibly guarding the entrance against anyone who wanted to interfere.

The path of decay was narrow, and here and there I saw normal booted footprints, as if someone else had walked down with them as well.

"Do you think a handler in human form came down here?" I asked Alitas as I pointed them out.

"Possibly. It would make sense if they wanted to take something." He frowned as he spoke, and it made me wonder again what someone might have been doing here or looking for.

As I reached the bottom of the steps, I realized that this wasn't a long, empty corridor after all. The walls were lined with graves. They were full of bones and decayed people, but they hadn't been touched or disrespected in any way.

"Catacombs," Ben said from behind me.

I still walked either side of the line of decay, but I didn't hold my hands out. There were too many holes in the walls with the dead in for me to want to reach out and touch.

As we went further along, we must have gone almost the full length of the building again when it turned a corner and doubled back. There were more bodies on this side, but it was as if these were more important people. They had little plaques or carvings attached to the walls beside them.

The lettering had been carved in wood and had worn out through time, so much so that many of them were unreadable. Further down again, the plaques became metal. These could still be read although I had to wipe dust off them. While I didn't want to touch the bodies in their resting places, I didn't mind wiping the debris of time from their nameplates.

I read a few before I realized these weren't human names. They were dragon names, along with their colors and ranks in some kind of dragon army.

"This must be the resting place of the dragons from this city. It was attacked by the demon the last time, but they stood their ground and were instrumental in helping to get him beneath the gate." Ben came closer and pointed out a name he recognized.

Not knowing what to think or do, I froze to the spot. How could we be under a human church in Denver but also in the crypt of a whole city of dragons?

"Do you think they had any idea when they built a church above this?" Flick's voice was gentle and respectful of the ancestors around us.

No one answered him. We had no way to know while we were down here. All we could do was keep following the trail and hope we got answers somewhere.

The shadow catchers had continued with no deviation in their path. Whatever they'd come down here for, it wasn't the long-dead bodies of dragons. I briefly wondered why they were all in human form and none as dragons until we reached a small alcove off to one side.

Two dragon skeletons sat in it, curled up around each other. The plaque for these two sat in the middle of the wall above, and I read it aloud. "Serene and Sebereth. Born and died together."

"Twins, I guess?" Neritas stepped in slightly so he could get a better look. They appeared to be smaller than us in dragon form, but curled up as they were with only their skeletons left, it was hard to tell. "They're young, not fully adults."

I shuddered and, ready to get out of there, continued down the path.

As it reached the end, it turned once more, but this time

at a right angle. As soon as I went around the corner, I gasped. The sight in front of me was stunning.

Instead of more rows of the dead, a large cavern went both downward from our position in one direction and slightly further up in the other. It was lit somehow magically, and I felt a faint power source with magic in the room.

Stepping down, I saw that the shadow catchers hadn't gone much further. They'd left a small, decayed patch a little way down but nothing beyond that. At least two had separated and worked back and forth, based on a groove that showed repeated travel. They had guarded here for a while.

In my mind's eye, I imagined a handler here looking around while they protected him. But that didn't help me work out what they'd come down here for.

I moved past their final line. At least three dragon skeletons rested in the cavern, and they were more like an adult-sized dragon. One of them was a lot bigger and made me feel small and inadequate, even as a dragon.

They seemed to be placed around something, but if they were protecting anything, it wasn't there now. I explored the whole thing, walking between ribs and under spines so I didn't miss any important details. When I was sure nothing was there, I pulled back to survey the place as a whole.

They all focused on a point in the middle of the cavern, an empty section of the floor. What had been here, and why was it so important that the demon had come here first and stolen it?

I walked to that spot, feeling with my mind for magic as

well as everything I could see. At the same time, I made myself brighter. Despite being tired and low on magical energy, I need to see properly.

Several footprints showed in the dust, but they stopped as if they'd reached a barrier or something solid. I crouched, my mind serving me next as I found the magical power source in the room. Closing my eyes, I connected to it. It felt similar to the pillars that had surrounded the gate, but not as powerful or as active.

I tried to feed it power and see if giving it some activated it. Nothing happened, but it tried to suck more magic out of me. I cut the connection, too weak to give it more than a tiny amount.

"I can't seem to get this to respond," I said aloud before I realized that no one else in the room could feel what I was feeling, with the exception of maybe Neritas.

He came over to me anyway, along with Alitas, Ben, and Flick. The rest kept guard in much the same way the shadow catchers had.

"Something in the floor?" Neritas asked. I nodded and pointed to where it was.

"I tried connecting to it and it wants to suck energy out of me like a thirsty man taking water from a pitcher."

"Do you want me to give it some?" he asked. The connection he had with his mind was already reaching out.

"Try taking some," Alitas suggested before I could confirm either way. "If Scarlet gave it some and it just tried to take more, but nothing happened, then try taking magic. Drain it the way the handler did to Scarlet's flying disks that one time."

I could have kicked myself for not being the one to

think of it, but Alitas had a point. The handler had made this work somehow. It was the only thing we had seen them do with magic.

Neritas connected, and I could see the strain as it tried to pull from him. He had to fight it. He wasn't used to magic resisting him.

Fearing for his safety, I tried to connect again. It hurt to stop it from pulling any magic from me, but I forced it to give up some and provide the same sort of connection that the island of the ancestors did, and it stopped fighting me and Neritas too.

His eyes widened as he sucked in the magic it gave out. I let him take some of it so he would be powered up, but I took the rest so I wouldn't be entirely devoid of magic. The device ran out, and it rumbled and pushed up through the floor like it was parting sand.

Something like a pedestal emerged, and bones radiated out from it, forming a cage around us and trapping Neritas and me within it. That was all. An empty dais and what amounted to a cage for someone who wouldn't be able to break out using non-magical means.

Here and there I saw signs of decay and some bones that had been snapped away. If this had once been a cage, the handler had broken it and slipped out, no doubt taking with him whatever had been inside.

I connected to the pedestal again and fed it a little magic. Almost immediately, it retreated. The earth shook as it receded into the ground and out of sight.

I exhaled and looked around. The demon had taken what he had come for and we hadn't been here to stop him. But it didn't make much sense either. If something had been hidden here, why had it been made easier for the shadow catchers and demons to get at than other dragons? What was special about it? And why had it been hidden in the first place?

We headed back out. I was exhausted and drained, and leaving with more questions than I had arrived with. And I still had to get back to Detaris somehow.

The person from the church was waiting right where we had left him. He looked up eagerly to see if we had answers.

"About all we can tell you is that the whole area under there is a dragon crypt from what used to be a dragon city," I said as he looked down there. "Seems safe enough now that the shadow catchers are gone, but I wouldn't trust it to lots of people. Take a look at the inside and then seal it back up again."

"You won't want to go back down there?" he asked. "If your kind are down there?"

"I don't know what they stood for or were trying to achieve, but there's nothing left for me and my people down there but bones." I gave him a wan smile and patted him on the shoulder again.

"I'm sorry."

"It's okay. You rest up and get better. I need to return to my people and see if I can find a record of this place and what might have been hidden here." I walked away before he could reply. I knew he would be all right. The demon wasn't coming back, and I had work to do.

As I stepped back out into the light again, I blinked several times.

The captain joined me. "You all right?"

"The demon stole a relic of the dragons that had been buried with our kind under the buildings here. I need to return to Detaris as swiftly as possible and see if I can find out what, and if it is capable of anything in particular. I don't know if he's trying to handicap me, stop me from putting him back behind the gate, or power himself." I told him everything so the information would be shared.

"Let me see if I can get you back there faster. You don't look as if you could fly right now."

"I can't," I said, confirming his assessment. "And neither can a lot of the dragons who came with me. Many of them were drained and stretched beyond themselves."

"You have my word that we'll look after anyone left behind and get them back to you as soon as we can as well. Least we can do for you flying all this way to help." The captain called around and told one of his squad to go get something I wasn't familiar with.

"I haven't really done much to help yet, so please don't get too comfortable."

"Not done much to help? You flew here as fast as you could and then drained yourself and every dragon with you to heal as many of our people as you could. You possibly saved every life left to save. And I get the impression that, had you any more magic to give, you wouldn't have stopped until everyone had been entirely healed." The captain saluted me. "You went above and beyond for people you didn't have to."

I gulped, grateful for someone who saw what I'd done and didn't hate me for trying and failing.

CHAPTER SEVEN

The strangeness of flying through the sky in a helicopter when I could have flown as a dragon didn't cease the entire time I was in there. The army hadn't agreed to take all of us, or all the way, but we were most of the way back to the city with the dragons who could recover fastest and fly the rest of the way. Everyone else was driving back to save their wings and rejoin us later.

Alitas, Ben, Flick, and Neritas were always at my side, and this time was no different. Jared and Jace were nearby too, making sure I didn't leave them behind.

The rest of my companions were those too determined to be left behind, like Capricia. I hadn't really talked to her much in the last few weeks. The friendship we had started trying to form had been shattered when she'd backed Grigick for the monarch of the dragon race.

I had thought her a friend and protector, and then she had not only betrayed that and spoken out against me, but had stood and watched as others had attacked me. Then she'd told the elders lies to get the city to turn against me as well. I still hadn't gotten to the bottom of her motivations.

When I'd proved that Grigick was not fit to lead the dragons and didn't have the power to stop the demon and fix the gate, Capricia had relinquished her goal. But it had cost us precious time and was one of several events that had prevented me from fixing the gate before the demon broke out.

Dwelling on what had once been would lead to madness, however, and I wouldn't entertain it. I needed to focus on the future and whatever it was the demon was up to now.

The captain moved closer so I could hear him over the din. "We're about five minutes away from landing."

I nodded.

"Open up a door or hatch and we'll fly from here." I motioned for the dragons with me to grab their gear and get ready.

Within a second Alitas was up on his feet and by my side, no doubt wanting to go first to keep me safe. I wasn't about to argue. Because we had got a lift with the military, I wasn't on the flight route I had expected and I didn't know what the right direction was. Once again, he would need to guide us.

In some ways, I knew I was making some large assumptions about Alitas. None of us had ever flown over the human cities unless under duress, and he was no more experienced than I was at navigating through the world. But he seemed far more confident, and being in the lead allowed him to make decisions to keep me safe.

Even if it was lazy of me, it was also what Alitas preferred. He wanted to be out in front.

When I saw a side door open, I got all the dragons on their feet, and we moved to the edge. The soldiers hung back, except for one who told us the dangers of jumping from a helicopter and how to make sure we didn't hit anything on the drop down from the vehicle.

I smiled to myself but nodded and let him talk. He'd soon see what was going to happen. All of us jumped off things regularly. A moving helicopter was something new, but none of us were fazed.

Alitas jumped and transformed, and I did the same, pushing away from the helicopter and letting myself drop enough that I could transform and then spreading my wings and powering up and ahead of our ride.

I wondered what the pilot thought of seeing dragons suddenly appearing and flying with him. Until everyone was out of the helicopter, we all fell in beside to wait, some of us ahead, others to the sides. They had gone from flying solo to flying for the first time with a huge dragon squadron.

I wondered if anyone on the ground below might be paying attention to get a photo of us all together, but we weren't flying that low and I doubted anyone would care.

Once every dragon was out, we lifted and cleared off the helicopter's flight path and then banked off to one side and onto the course we needed for Detaris. It wasn't a huge distance away now, but I knew we would be in the air for at least a few more hours. It was also getting late, and the sun was slowly setting ahead of us.

Although it was hard to look in that direction for too

long, it was beautiful and was a welcome sight to encourage our tired bodies toward home. We flew hard and fast, and I wondered if somewhere the demon was also flying toward a specific location. Or was he resting?

I had no way to know. I hadn't worried about what he was doing, really, until today, and now it was all I could think about. I couldn't let him stay this far ahead of me. We had to figure out what he was doing and where he would be next and get ahead of it. I didn't want to wait for the next massacre and only turn up in time to heal the wounded.

By the time Detaris came into view, I was exhausted and had been pulling on the magical connection I had with the island of the ancestors to spread the little bit of magic out to everyone and help them along.

We flew lower and through the protective field before too many of the humans on the outside of the force field saw us and caused a fuss. The rest of our dragons were going to be on the next flight back and would take their time to fly closer. Kryos had stayed with them, although he wasn't entirely happy about being left behind himself.

The elders and my mother flew to us and met us in the air.

Where is everyone? my mother asked.

They're all safe, I sent to everyone. *They've paused to rest while we flew back faster with news, but none of the dragons came to any harm or saw any fighting. We were too late.*

It seems you have a story to tell. Come, rest while we're informed and let us get you sustenance. Brenta flew up and used her agility to get ahead of my tired and slow group.

Although Brenta's brusque efficiency and ability to go

straight to the point was sometimes annoying when I was on the interrogation end of her intent, in situations like this it got people cared for fast and effectively. She was a useful woman to have around in a crisis.

I encouraged everyone else up to the elders' tower ahead of me to make sure they were all safe. Plenty of other dragons followed us, not wanting to be left out of the conversations about what had happened. I considered shutting the hatches so we could talk in private, but they deserved to know as well.

We would do this publicly so they could all be part of the discussion.

I changed as I touched down and put my bag down right by the exit, ready to pick it up at a moment's notice. Alitas and Flick were the first to my side but Neritas was swiftly after, bearing a plate full of my favorite foods.

"Eat while everyone who wants to hear the news gathers. This might take a while."

I wasn't going to argue. I was more hungry than I cared to admit. Ben approached me next and leaned in to whisper in my ear.

"I'm going to the library. Something is bugging me and I want to go check it out as soon as I can. If I'm right, it will help."

Although I wanted to stop him and call him back to the meeting, I nodded and let him go. It wasn't like him to not be at my side for something like this, so it must be important.

My mother stayed by my side, giving me a large one-armed hug. I held onto her for a fraction of a second longer, feeling the warmth and appreciating that someone was so pleased to see me.

After being scared to come back to the city for a long time, it was a change to feel welcome, wanted, and cared for by everyone, even if only a few had shown it so far.

I ate while everyone gathered, wolfing down as much food as I thought I could get away with. It didn't take long for the balconies to be full of dragons in human form, with more in dragon form holding onto parts of towers or circling so they could try to listen.

Although the entire city couldn't listen to what we said, I wanted to give them a chance to get themselves in some kind of order and be present to listen.

Over the next half an hour, I told them what had happened, what I'd found, and what I thought it might mean. I spent some time talking about how hurt humanity had been and that they had paid heavily for us not being prepared for the attack. The moment I paused, the elders threw questions at me.

They were as concerned as I was about the birds that had turned on the humans in huge numbers. I couldn't blame them for being scared by it either. We'd been fighting shadow catchers and the occasional handler for ages. Now there was something new. Some kind of corrupted wildlife. It was a scary thought.

Although I'd told the story candidly so the elders would understand what was going on and the seriousness of it, I had left out some minor details on the extent of the damage to the humans and how healing them had drained every single dragon I had with me.

I didn't want to cause a panic, only give them an idea

that this was a serious problem that could threaten all of us and those we cared about. Not an easy distinction to make and follow.

Before I got much further, Ben returned. He had what looked to be a very old book in his hands, and the librarian I had once clashed with in tow. She hurried after him with her glasses perched on the end of her nose and a look of great annoyance on her face.

"I found it," he declared. "A description of what was probably taken."

Ben held the book aloft so all could see it for a few seconds and then came to the main table laid out in front of the elders. He splayed it out, fixing it on a certain page with the gentlest of touches before looking up at everyone.

"When the demon was trapped behind the gate, the magical world all came together and put all their resources into defeating him. They had a set of items...artifacts perhaps, that, when close together, could make the dragon weaker and help them to drive him back. Once they had achieved their goal, they dismantled it and spread it out among the dragon cities best equipped to protect it at the time."

"Does it say why they felt the need to do so?" Brenta asked, voicing a thought I'd had but not wanted to utter.

"I believe they didn't want these powerful artifacts to ever be used on anyone else. They could have been used to control other dragons or humanity, and it was considered too much of a temptation."

Everyone nodded. Although, as far as I was aware, no ruler had ever gone full dictator and slaughtered anyone, the dragon race hadn't been perfect by a long way. I was fairly sure I would have made the same decision and put something that powerful out of the reach of any single person.

I thought for a moment as everyone muttered in small groups and talked about the pictures on the page. It wasn't a single artifact, but it was clear they were a set—some gauntlets, a circlet similar to a crown, and what looked like a lance.

"Which part do we think he has already?" I asked. "Is there a log of the items and where they are kept?"

Ben shook his head and the librarian beside him frowned, which made it clear she didn't know of anything that could help me.

"Look anyway. For any mention of these, in anything. What they can do, where they might be, how many parts, when they were handed out. It's all information that can give us direction and understanding." I took out my phone as I spoke and carefully took photos of every page with a picture or description that would be useful.

There wasn't a lot in the book—just pictures and basic information that it had been used against the demon to trap him before being split up. Everything I already knew, but it was a start and it gave me an idea of what the demon might be up to. He was gathering the parts before I collected them to use against him.

"This is a very serious situation," Brenta said as the librarian and Ben left, taking the book with them.

It was an obvious statement, but I could understand her voicing it. We needed to figure this out and stop the demon before he gathered too many, but I was flying blind and he had clearly known where to find at least one of them.

"Can we also find old maps of the dragon world and all our cities? From right after the demon was trapped behind the gate until the city in Denver died out. Let us also gather information on tours the red dragons did, if possible." I looked at Alitas as I said this last part, hoping that the captains of the honor guard through the years might have kept records of these sorts of things.

He nodded as if it might be something he could sort out for me, but it wouldn't do me much good if I couldn't narrow it down another way.

Somehow, I had to figure this out, and I had very little to go on and no one I could turn to for advice.

With no more thoughts or plans coming to mind, I called the meeting to an end and sent everybody back to their homes for now. We couldn't do anything else.

Before Brenta would let me leave, she insisted we talk about the logistics of me being in charge of the city. She gave me some messages from the elders of other cities. They were also scared and worried, and some thanked me for letting the world know we existed as I had said I would.

Not needing to hide everything allowed the cities closest to humanity to stop focusing so much of their time and effort on keeping secrets and instead switch to interacting with the people around them and trading more openly.

It had shocked people that dragons existed and to find that they had been selling us food or other goods for a long time, but most had taken it well and even been enthusiastic. Some clamored to be the ones to provide services to us. Already certain companies were approaching me to set up shops and restaurants in our cities. I ignored all of it for now. It was crazy to think about commerce and capitalism when the fate of the entire world might be at stake in another way.

As soon as I could, I left as well, wanting to rest and think for a while. I could only do so much in one day, no matter how much damage the demon did. If I didn't recharge, I didn't have a hope of stopping him anyway.

CHAPTER EIGHT

Each new day seemed to bring with it a fresh set of challenges. Once again, by the time I was sitting with my friends at breakfast, there were new messages to respond to and more news articles to be aware of.

Not all of the world was responding well to finding out that dragons, magic, and other things like it existed. Over breakfast, my friends showed me some of the many videos, news articles, and clippings about dragons or me.

On some level, I knew that these people didn't know me, but the criticism from total strangers still stung. I wasn't perfect, but at every point, I tried to do my best.

No matter how I felt, however, I had to push it aside and focus on the bigger picture. We needed to find the demon and work out how to capture him again.

Jace was off working with the dragons who wanted to fight, training and teaching them what we had learned already, and Kryos had gone with her to see if any would make good honor guards. I wanted to be with them, learning, practicing, and seeing how much power was there, but I had no choice but to stay where I was.

Ben and Reijo had spent all night at the library working together to find any and all information they could. Both of them were enjoying it. They had gone with me everywhere, and gladly, but the two of them were in their element surrounded by books. I imagined Anthony would have loved being with them in that way too.

Griffin acted as my liaison with the elders of the city, and the elders corresponded with dragons of other cities. After fighting with the elders and finding I didn't get along very well with them in the past, I found myself relying on them more and more as they gave advice, helped, and navigated the tricky politics with people on every continent under the sun.

If I thought about everything too much, I froze, overwhelmed by the enormity of tracking down my enemy, protecting a planet I couldn't travel around fast enough, and navigating the politics as the leader of an entire, scattered race. It was my fault for wanting the world to know about us and agreeing to be in charge, but I still felt overwhelmed.

"What are you going to do about the demon?" Anna asked, looking over at me after yet another video had finished. This one had been clips of all the badass fights I had been in publicly.

I shrugged, aware that I didn't have a plan yet and needed to form one. "I can't be everywhere at once, so until we can find a location to try and protect, or go to it so we can collect the artifacts he's after, all I can do is train and prepare others."

Neritas gave me a look as I finished speaking. I knew he was thinking of the powers he was now gaining. We might be able to do more there, but it was something I didn't fully understand, so from that point of view, it was an unreliable tactic. If any color dragon could learn how to harness the abilities that until now had been red dragon only, what had changed? Had my color line been hiding the secret that all could do it?

I shuddered at the thought and excused myself from the company of my friends. I needed to help in some way, but my options were slim and didn't make me feel much better about the future. As Neritas and Flick fell in beside me and Alitas led the way, I knew one thing was for sure: I wasn't alone.

The honor guards knew that Neritas and Flick could control the magic as well, and feed it, so I had agreed to try to teach more of them. I trusted them, even if I wasn't ready for the entire race to know.

Alitas led us up the beach from the city, keeping us in the bubble that meant we couldn't be seen by the humans lining the cliff and around the city in general, but far enough away from most of the city that no one would be able to work out what we were doing exactly.

Neritas had already been explaining to Alitas how to connect to the magic, but it was very different to talk about than practice. When Alitas was ready, I connected to his magic, creating the threads and moving them around to show him what to do.

Although he wasn't as swift as Neritas to understand and be able to take over from me, within about fifteen minutes he was able to work on his own under my supervision.

I had to explain a lot more than I had with either Flick or Neritas, as the captain was full of questions, but I didn't tire of them. Of everything I was doing, this felt as if it prepared us all best for what the future might hold.

We hadn't been working together for much longer when Capricia flew down toward us. I saw the curiosity in her eyes as she studied us, but we stopped linking our magic when she got close so she wouldn't be able to tell what had been happening. We were simply sitting in the sand, away from the city.

"Is there more news?" I asked her, getting to my feet. If she had come out here to get me, then something important had happened.

"It's the humans. They've sent one of their commanders to speak with you. Something about needing your help. Elders thought you ought to handle this one or at least input into his questions."

I nodded and quickly followed her, my three friends and guards quickly forming up around us.

"Shall we invite him into the city?" Alitas asked me.

"He's already asked that you meet him in the tent they used for your broadcast and diplomatic meetings." Capricia looked apologetic, as if she didn't think anyone should have agreed to that without consulting me first, but I thought it was better. As much as I liked having my friends in the city, inviting politicians and military personnel in was another matter.

I went back into the center of the city to allow Alitas to

select the dragons he thought ought to come with me for safety, and immediately Jace spotted us.

"I'm coming with you," she said after I explained where I was going.

"Good," Alitas replied before I could. "You'll take no shit from anyone."

For a reason I couldn't explain, I already felt better. When Griffin flew down and informed me he would also join my delegation, I felt even calmer. Griffin could handle politics.

By the time the combination of volunteers and guards Alitas wanted had assembled, I had a group of fifteen and felt more prepared for whatever might follow. I'd also donned the majority of my armor. Although I didn't expect trouble, it was important to be ready in case the demon attacked again. I would drop everything to go fight him if I could.

On top of that, my mother came and put the small human crown that had been designed for me on my head. It was simple, something I had insisted on, but I wasn't sure I wanted to wear it now.

"One of the things your father said to me was that you gain respect when you look the part you're supposed to play. They will treat you like a queen if you look like a queen."

I still wasn't convinced, but if my father had given the advice, I was inclined to follow it, even if I didn't understand why.

My mother stepped away, and I informed the elders that she was in charge of Detaris until my return. Everyone was waiting for me. I looked at all of them, grateful to have them standing beside me again.

We walked out of the city, all in human form, not wanting to scare anyone. If nothing else, I hoped it would encourage people to see us as enough like them that we weren't treated like aliens.

Several military personnel met me, many of them armed and ready for combat.

"Good afternoon," I said, as friendly as I could be. The unit commander greeted me in response.

"I'm Lieutenant Douglas, ma'am." He saluted.

I hadn't expected the greeting or the military, but I nodded my respect. I knew these men and women would be following orders and hoping for the best, like most of the dragons with me.

"It's a pleasure to meet you and your unit, Lieutenant. Please, call me Scarlet." I realized as I spoke that it was a very informal offer and in direct contradiction to what I had been advised by my mother. "Lead the way to wherever I'm needed."

He didn't give any indication of how he felt about the request but motioned for me to follow him before his unit fell in beside us and acted as an extra escort layer.

It was strange to have so many people around me, some for my protection and some possibly to protect others from me. Not that they could really prevent me from doing whatever I wanted to. It was fine by me for them to think they could, however, and so I let them do whatever made them feel safe around me.

I wanted this to work. For all of us to work together

and not feel threatened. All I wanted was to stop the demon before anyone else got hurt, human or dragon.

We were led into the same tent as last time, but the inside had changed. Sections had been divided up by fabric, although a central corridor ran through the main section and several tables with electronic monitoring, surveillance, and maps of the tactical military kind had been added. People in military uniforms were either working at stations or hurrying here and there on various tasks.

It had clearly become a temporary military outpost and instantly I felt uncomfortable. Did they see us as a threat?

There were some familiar faces among the personnel, and a few smiled or nodded at me in recognition. I returned the gestures, trying to show ease and calm. I didn't want to make anything worse if we were on dodgy ground.

"Please wait here while I check if the general is ready for you."

I raised an eyebrow at the cheek of being asked to wait for a general, but I wasn't about to make a huge fuss. The soldier in front of me was following his orders and I was an unknown queen of a nation of people not entirely recognized whose land was now under dispute in a lot of places.

Thankfully, whoever this general was, he didn't keep me waiting. I heard a deep, rough-sounding voice through the canvas barriers between makeshift offices. "Don't waste our time. Have the dragon warrior shown in and let us get on with the important matters."

"Yes, sir," Lieutenant Douglas replied.

Before he came back to us, I led my delegation deeper into the tent and toward the sound of the voice, to make it clear that we'd heard everything. As the lieutenant pushed back the canvas to ask us to come inside, I swept past him and into the general's office.

Thankfully, it was a decent-sized area without much furniture in it, so the fourteen dragons with me could all follow, although we took up a lot of space inside the office on this side of the desk.

The general was a tall man, built well, with not an ounce of fat on him. He surveyed all of us as he strode around the desk to shake my hand.

"I'm General Miller. How would you like to be addressed, Your Highness? I understand that you're a queen, but I don't know your customs."

I was stunned by the courtesy and respect with which he spoke. Along with the speed in which he'd invited me in, it made me feel considerably better about working with him, and I considered the answer to that question before beginning to explain what I thought would be most helpful.

"In all honesty, General, I don't know what our customs are either. The line of royalty was broken between me and my father. He died long before anyone, including myself, knew that there would be another heir to the throne, and it has stood empty for a long time. I think Your Highness would suffice for now, however."

Although I had considered suggesting he call me Scarlet as I had the lieutenant, I opted to follow my mother's advice this time and stick with holding my rank and expecting to be treated as a queen.

"It sounds as if life hasn't been easy for you, Your Highness, but you have my respect, both as a warrior and as a leader. One of the requirements of my job has led to me watching a lot of clips of your battles. You have skill, and the care you show those who fight alongside you is clear. I hope you understand that I am here with the same desire in my heart—to protect those in my care and fight any enemy we may have."

I nodded, feeling the sentiment and hoping it was true. So much distrust of authority had grown in my life that I instinctively didn't want to believe him. Anyone could say anything. Showing it was another matter.

"Thank you, General. I appreciate your saying so. I hope you don't consider this rude, but can we get on with the matter at hand? You have asked for me to come to you and I have done so, but my city needs me and I am eager to do everything I can to find the demon that attacked Denver and stop him from attacking anyone or anywhere else."

"That's why I asked you here. I imagine that you are already doing everything the dragons are capable of, but I would like to give my people more tools to defend us as well. I've seen the debriefs with those soldiers and police who have fought alongside you, and how you seemed to apply some sort of..." The general didn't finish, unable to find the word.

"Magic. A charge of it, to be more precise," I offered as a description.

"Yes, a charge. That enabled us to harm these enemies."

"It's a combination of the power and magic that builds up in all the different colors of dragons in our cities. When more and more different colors are combined, it becomes more potent and deadly to the demons. We naturally generate it over time, but I can also draw small amounts from the ancestors of my kind. In the battles you have seen me in, I have added this magical energy to the surface of bullets, shields, and armor, and even one of your planes."

Alitas shifted as I spoke, almost as if he was uncomfortable with what I'd said. I wasn't sure what element had bothered him, or if he was trying to draw my attention to something else, but I stopped speaking.

The general had nodded along to my explanation and listened as I talked, but he motioned for me to sit before he replied.

"I would like to discuss this more, if you're willing to hear my request and help me to understand. I can have lunch brought here and see that all your…delegation is also taken care of." General Miller looked pointedly up at the dragons standing around me.

"Some of them will remain with me. I hope you understand, General, but I'm the last surviving royal, and none of my people want a repeat of having no leader. I have four other dragons with me at all times."

"Of course, Your Highness. I can understand the desire they have to ensure your safety. The rest can be nearby, as you wish. There's another tent set up just behind this one that we're using as a canteen, and they're welcome to patrol the area as well, if they need to look out for these demons for us. I've also picked up on there being some way you can all detect them coming."

"Yes, my color dragon is needed to both harness the magic of others and to sense the enemies approaching." I didn't like to perpetuate a lie, but not every dragon knew the truth yet and I wasn't about to confess a secret to a human general when I hadn't told my own people.

The general paused, frowning briefly before he called for Lieutenant Douglas to come back and escort those I didn't need to stay to the canteen and show them where they could patrol and protect us all.

I kept Neritas, Flick, Alitas, and Jace, despite the latter not being one of my honor guards.

As General Miller requested lunch for all of us, I realized that I was having my very first political and military strategy-based meeting with humanity, and this could shape the entire future of how we cooperated and fought together.

I'd better not screw this up.

CHAPTER NINE

With a full plate of food, a soda, and the ease of being able to sit down and focus on something else, I gave my attention back to the matter at hand.

Lunch with General Miller had only just begun and that meant it wouldn't be long before we began talking about our future cooperation with each other. The general hadn't asked me yet if I could power more of his weapons, but he'd said enough that I could connect the dots. What else would a man like him want, knowing what I was capable of, but to help his soldiers protect humanity?

I nibbled on my sandwiches, patiently waiting for the general to get to his point. I was curious how he would lead up to it and how much information he would try to get out of me first. Although I liked this man so far, liking him and trusting him with everything about the dragon world and our magic were two different things.

Of course, I recognized that as a problem of my own making and I tried to push past the habitual response I'd learned from the life I'd led so far, and act in a more logical manner. In this case, I wasn't inclined to risk the danger to my own race by being too trusting too fast.

"Thank you for giving me your time, Your Highness," General Miller said after he had also sampled a small sandwich and sat back.

"You have me curious enough, and also have my complete willingness to work together in ways that can see our common enemy defeated. Tell me what you wish for so we can see what is possible and what might still be done." I deliberately sounded commanding, not wanting to waste time if it could be helped, and wanting the general to understand that I would only entertain so much beating around the bush.

"Would you charge our weaponry and armor as you do your own? We wish to fight as well, and it is clear that we cannot do so without your help."

I was impressed with his directness, though I had clearly encouraged it. I was pleased to know I had guessed right, and now I gave his request a little more thought. When in battle, I had never hesitated to charge their weapons and equipment, endowing them as well as my own people. It allowed everyone to fight to the best of their ability.

Outside of a fight, it was different, however.

"I know that it requires energy from you and your people, and it isn't something that can be done without the presence of a dragon. It's not an automatic process, from what I've heard you say, but our understanding of this process is basic and relies on what we've seen you do in the past."

Maybe it would be best if he had a little demonstration.

"It does require energy from a group, yes, and I am willing to charge up the weapons and armor in this camp to help you understand. I can do so easily enough if they are brought before me and I can see the items needed."

The general called for Lieutenant Douglas again and instructed him to have every weapon, round of ammo, and piece of armor brought to the storage area in three waves for each shift of soldiers.

I exhaled, wondering how much I had signed up to charge. The camp had appeared small enough from the city, but had I missed some of them?

Despite my fears and the questions I now had running through my head, I didn't voice any of them and focused on eating instead. We ate as the general handled the chaos his command created and ate as well.

"Thank you," he said to me as soon as his attention was no longer being stolen elsewhere. "It means a lot to us that you would be so easily willing."

I didn't reply, sensing more coming. I continued eating my lunch.

"This…energy…you charge with. It comes from all of you somehow?"

"Yes. Magic is a simple word for it," I replied, wondering if he would use the word. The corner of my mouth twitched up when his gaze met mine and he frowned at the suggestion. He didn't want to call it magic.

"It's a connection we have to the world around us. The way we live generates it. Some of us more than others."

"And dragons of your color funnel this energy?"

"To put it simply, yes." I shrugged as if it wasn't a huge deal, but I could sense the direction of his line of questioning. He wanted to assess exactly what we were capable of. To him, we were an unknown force, and therefore a danger as much as a powerful ally.

"Could this be repeated by other dragons in other areas of the country? In case this demon attacks cities on the other side of the US. I know you responded as fast as you could, and flew all the way to Denver the second you heard of the demon showing up there, but—"

"I wasn't fast enough," I finished the sentence for him, knowing what he saw as the problem. "I cannot put into words how I felt at putting everything I and the dragons with me had into getting there to fight and finding we were too late to do more than heal the wounded."

"You prevented many more deaths that day, and you have our gratitude. I hope you know that." For a second, the air of this meeting being a negotiation vanished from the conversation and I felt like I might be talking to one of my own friends and confidants, like Ben, my mother, or Reijo. It didn't last, however.

"Thank you," I replied. I noticed he had finished eating as well. "Shall we go to your storage so I can begin the process?"

I got up, despite having phrased my words like a question. If he wanted me to do this as much as I suspected, there wasn't going to be any kind of delay, and we could get on with it without me having to answer any more of his questions.

The general took the prompt and hurriedly got to his feet as well before leading me to the armory himself. It wasn't in this main tent either, and we all went outside, where I called to my company of dragons. It drew a questioning look from our escort.

"This is easier and kinder on us if I draw from all of them and not only a few. The closer we all are the better. I would appreciate having them all in close proximity when we do this. The majority can wait just outside."

"I understand." General Miller led me a little way into the trees, where a more solid structure had already been erected and secured. In front of it, a small group of soldiers was already lined up behind Lieutenant Douglas. I was relieved to see that there were only twelve of them and they were all holding magazines in one hand and guns in the other.

Wanting to show my cooperation, I connected to the dragons around me and drew magic from the isle of the ancestors, and a little from the sword at my waist and the shield attached to my rucksack. Within a second I had what I needed to reach out and, one by one, charge the weapons.

I didn't need physical contact, but I acted as if I did and reached out to each set of items. I placed my hands on them in turn as I charged them up.

Although I didn't want to make it look as easy as it was, I still didn't want to waste too much time, so I moved swiftly from one to the next until all twelve soldiers were carrying charged weaponry. Then, without being asked, I slowly reached out and touched Lieutenant Douglas's gun, the weapon holstered at his side.

I charged that as well. The process was very fast with only a few bullets.

"There. Everything out here is charged and ready to

damage any kind of demon that might threaten you all." I looked toward the storage to indicate I was ready to move on to everything in there.

"That was fast. Is it entirely charged?" General Miller asked as he walked toward the armory anyway.

"It's either charged or not, in this case. It will do what's needed, but a single contact from a demon will use up the charge. That's not a problem with bullets, but the armor, fabric, and everything else like that will only repel a demon once and cause damage. And contact from a demon with no protection is not recommended under any circumstances."

The general shook his head. "Denver made that very clear."

He took a key from his pocket and unlocked the door. I moved to his side as he opened it, letting my other dragons know not to crowd the area. Alitas came up behind and to one side of me, and Neritas and Flick were a little behind him. They made it clear they were there to keep an eye on me and stay between me and possible dangers.

I didn't go inside the armory but leaned in enough to see everything.

Making it look as if I could move the charge through other objects, I put a hand on the outside walls on each side of the door and concentrated. Once again, I charged all the bullets, blades, grenades, and every piece of armor I could identify in the armory. I was shocked by how much was in here, but a heated battle with the kind of numbers that had turned up at Denver could drain the resources in here in a very short space of time.

It took me a little longer to charge all this, but I did it as fast and as thoroughly as I could before stepping back.

By the time I was done, the lieutenant had dismissed the twelve waiting soldiers with their charged weaponry, and twelve more were coming up to stand in their stead.

I still felt good and had magic to draw on, but I paused and exhaled.

"Thank you," the general said again as he locked the armory.

"I hope you don't have to use it in a hurry," I replied.

"That is what everyone hopes, but it is good to be prepared and have what might be needed."

"I fought hard to try and ensure nothing like this would ever be needed." I was unable to keep the bitterness from my voice at having failed. I knew I'd tried a lot of different options, continued to fight, and had come close to securing the gate. But I would never be able to stop questioning if I could have done more, or if someone was to blame and if lives could have been saved along the way.

"This will help us to help you. To hopefully end this before it gets any worse." He lifted his chin, determined and eager to prove that they could handle themselves, and I saw the pride he had in his strength and the strength of the military personnel under his command.

I moved to the new clutch of twelve soldiers and charged their equipment as well. After they were dismissed, I retreated a few steps toward the protective group of my friends as if I was tired and seeking comfort.

I wasn't worn out, but I had used enough energy from all of us to notice it. I wasn't used to charging this much at once outside of a battle. In those situations, I often drew magic from other sources more than the dragons, sources I slowly filled back up the rest of the time. But none of this equipment could hold extra charges.

No one spoke until the final soldier's weapons had also been charged and I was done with everything I had promised to charge.

"There. I have aided you in all the ways I can for now," I said as General Miller dismissed the last of his men and sent them back to their usual duties.

"Once again, you have our gratitude. I won't deny that I also hoped to have your agreement to see more of our resources powered up with the energy you create as well. This will be enough for my small team here to aid you in any battles near your city, but not anywhere else in the country."

I frowned. He was right, and I needed to concede something and agree to a process of charging more of their gear. The question was, how much was I willing to build up for them?

"I've done a lot today, but I could do something like this once a week perhaps, or half as much twice a week."

It was the general's turn to show his displeasure.

"So little? If this demon attacks even once a month, we would never be able to have enough."

"Once it is charged, it will always be charged, and I will always charge the weaponry of anyone fighting alongside me in the heat of battle as well. Do not fear for any soldiers in battle running out when a dragon is nearby. This can all be taken from here and sent somewhere further afield if it would serve your purposes better."

"That would definitely help." The general paused,

studying me for a few seconds. "But it doesn't give us enough. Are there other dragons who could assist you? Perhaps in other locations?"

"I wish it were that simple. But as far as I am aware, there are only three dragons left in the entire world who have the same color scales as I do, one of whom will never leave the safety of the most secure dragon city we have, and the other nowhere near as powerful as I am."

"I see," General Miller replied.

"My power is not unlimited, and neither is my time. I must consider many ways to combat these demons, but I am also needed to protect and aid my own people. Don't misunderstand my reluctance as anything but the complications of having multiple demands on me to act. I want this demon stopped before he grows too powerful. It is in my interests to work with you, as it is in yours to work with me."

I slowly walked away from the storage to the edge of the trees and the road that ran parallel to Detaris, giving the general no choice but to walk with me if he wanted to keep talking. Lieutenant Douglas came with us, but he kept a little way back, matching the position Alitas took on my flank with the general.

"I understand a little better now. For now, we would like to take your gracious offer. It is far better than nothing, and if, as you have explained, it is all permanent and you have asked for nothing in return, we will consider it a gift more than worth having. Perhaps there is a way we could return the favor, or aid your people in some way to give you more room to help us."

Although I could respect the general for not giving up

on getting what he wanted, I couldn't easily answer his question, nor was I sure that a trade would work with my people.

"I'll put the offer before my elders, the representatives of the dragons in each of the major cities, and see if something can be worked out. For now, that is the best I can offer."

The general bowed and thanked me for my time, officially ending our meeting by the time I was level with the main tent again. I was almost sorry to see him go as he walked away, taking the lieutenant with him back to his office.

I watched him go for a couple of seconds before I left to return to Detaris as well. If I had more dragons to aid in drawing magic, a good deal more could easily be made. Several of my cities were struggling for food, and it made sense to have weapons around the country that had the ability to hurt the demons if they showed up.

For the dragon world, it could easily be a trade that benefited us in both ways. But I didn't have the red dragons I needed, and so far, only two other dragons could truly help me—and they were both sworn to secrecy for now. It was a dilemma I needed to solve.

Both for us and for the sake of humanity.

CHAPTER TEN

Back in Detaris, I flew up to my tower and slipped into a seat before I said a word to anyone. Griffin had heard everything and made it clear he thought I had handled the meeting well and that he appreciated me not promising too much without consulting the elders.

"It's a shame we can't do more," I replied. "It would be good to have the humans able to defend themselves and buy us time to get to them. Or other dragons who might be closer."

"And we should equip our dragons with charged weaponry and armor too," Jace pointed out. "Wherever they are in the world."

I caught the tone of her voice and knew it was something her group of dragons had wanted to see since the beginning: all dragons given what they needed and allowed to have access to all the information and equipment. She had never liked the idea that the Detaris elders were hiding so much.

Until I had begun uncovering everything, it had never

occurred to her or the dragons with her that the elders hadn't realized how much of our history had been altered and forgotten either.

After filling my mother in on everything, as well as the elders, I was able to think through a plan of action to follow and what I wanted to do next.

"Let us put out a message to all the dragon cities asking for volunteers to fight again. I was doing that before the demon broke loose, and now they will know the seriousness of the situation. When we start to get ideas of the number of volunteers, let us start sending out charged items of our own. Anything of our own we send out, as opposed to the weaponry we give the human soldiers, will at least last longer than one use."

"I'll work with one of your elders to make it happen," Jace offered. Her offer of cooperation was a surprise that had half the room in shock.

"I'd be honored to help in this way and encourage the elders in other places to aid us," Brenta replied, adding to the hopeful atmosphere. Of all the people in the city to offer to work with Jace, she was the one I least expected. But she was the one that the other elders communicated with most, and that made her the perfect pairing.

They wasted no time, Jace following Brenta over to the elders' chambers, leaving me to focus on the next task I wanted to tackle.

"I'm going to need a schedule of what to charge when. Something that spreads out the requirements across each day so I can expend a little energy regularly," I said. "I can't risk exhausting every last drop with the demon on the loose."

"Leave that with me," my mom replied. "I'll make sure the soldiers are included, as well as our own supplies."

"I can help with being the liaison with the camp outside Detaris and see what else we can ask them for, especially for the cities that are struggling." Griffin got up again to go off and work with my mother on it.

I considered what else I could do. Until I was ready to tell the city that any dragon could harness the powers red dragons could, I had to be careful. We needed to charge as much as we could, but I didn't want to cause total chaos in the dragon community, especially when I didn't fully understand that aspect of magic yet.

"Can we contact Grigick and ask him if he'll also charge whatever he can? Either bring him here or send him items to charge?" Keeping in touch with him hadn't been at the top of my priorities when we'd last parted ways.

"I can see if he'll help," Capricia responded, giving me a very brief bow.

By the time I had dealt with the other small details around the city, I was exhausted and ready to sleep for a week. I wasn't going to get the chance, however. While I considered my options, I made a mental note to go and get what was left of that stash of items and gear by the gate, assuming they were still there and the area hadn't been compromised when the tunnels had collapsed on me or when the demon had broken out.

Before I had a chance to talk to Alitas, Flick, and Neritas about this extra skill they had, Ben flew in. He transformed back into human form and rushed over to me to show me another book he'd found.

"This isn't a complete solution, but there's a sort of old

diary from a dragon involved in politics who was alive at the time the artifact was split up."

"He mentions it?" I hoped that if nothing else, it would give us a time window for when the pieces had been hidden.

"Yes. Some of them. And a rough area for where two of the pieces went."

I got up as Ben put the diary down on the dining table and gingerly opened the pages. It was written in the dragon language that I had recently begun learning and wasn't great at understanding yet. It was also in a script that was so ornate, and the ink so faded that it was a miracle Ben could read it at all.

"Here, he talks about going with a delegation who were flying east and how the king was accompanying them to the East Coast of the continent, and then how the king was going to continue to the next land to make sure the artifact was delivered into the correct hands and dealt with to his satisfaction."

While Ben read, I found my mind wandering to thoughts of what it must have been like to fly around and not worry about being seen, and to have the confidence of knowing that the demon was safe behind a gate and your job was done. All you had to do was make sure that dragons continued to live in peace and powered the gate now and then.

It struck me that it had also been this king's choice to separate out the parts and hide them in the first place. They must have been considered very dangerous as one item.

"Does it give any more detail about the cities they ended up in?" I asked. "'The next land' is pretty broad."

"A small amount more. I think it means somewhere in Europe for one of them. Not Africa. It talks about the land being covered in snow at this time of year and how it had been a long time since he'd last seen snow."

I nodded, agreeing with the logic that snow was much more likely to mean Europe than Africa, but it still left a pretty big area.

"That gives us a snowy region at this time of year in Europe, at the rough point in history detailed in the diary. Given that there aren't as many dragon cities over in Europe as there are here, all that information together could give us a few options that aren't far apart." Ben grinned and sat, clearly pleased with himself.

As I had done many times before, I reached over and gave his hand a squeeze. I might not have felt like I'd done much with my day besides talk to people, but all of the little things we had achieved so far added up and I could feel we were getting closer to our goals. With this many people helping me and all of us taking elements that played to our strengths, we stood a chance.

Despite this, I couldn't help the sweeping sense of foreboding that this wasn't going to be as easy as I hoped. The demon had been crafty, and I was still on my back foot.

With this information in mind, Ben promised to look up the cities and work with another of the elders who kept the records of the cities' populations and locations—a census of sorts. Between all the bits of information, perhaps we would get a destination I could get to first.

I was alone with Neritas, Flick, and Alitas after that, all three of them sticking around to talk to me.

"We need to consider training as many dragons as we can to control this magic," Alitas said as soon as he could be sure we wouldn't be overheard.

"I agree. But it's going to cause panic." I looked at the three of them, wondering if they had any suggestions on how we could explain it to everyone.

This wasn't going to be easy, and I feared the chaos it would cause. As much as I wanted to come clean, it was still an awful time to do so.

"It's possible that we can start teaching some of the other dragons. Start being strategic with whom we tell and whom we help." Neritas looked thoughtful. "That way, when the news about this gets out, we can say that we weren't keeping a secret and were passing the knowledge on in a controlled fashion that would make the dragon race stronger and more prepared to hold off the demon attacks."

"To let people know that we didn't want to cause chaos but were still sharing the knowledge as widely as it made sense to," I added, hoping it was the right course of action.

"I've tried to keep my counsel to myself in the past with your father and every other guard job I've had before that. My job is to serve and protect without a full understanding of anything, but, in this instance, I think this cannot be shared with the dragon population without a significant appreciation for the response." Alitas let his shoulders slump. He didn't want me to keep it a secret any more than I wanted to.

"Let us also look for a good way to tell everyone. Make

plans, put it in writing somewhere, and make sure that I am held accountable for this decision. Help me find the right time to tell people, and in the meantime, the right dragons to tell and train."

"I've been thinking about that last part. It would help to have dragons in other places trained to do this more than dragons here," Flick replied. "But we need dragons we can train here to go out and train others, so I think we need to pick a few dragons here who want to travel next."

"What about Jared?" Neritas asked. "We know he cares, and he's skilled and dedicated."

I approved without hesitation. Jared was a perfect choice. "Neritas, you teach him what you know as soon as you can."

"I would like leave to continue training and teaching the honor guards I choose. It's my job to protect you more than to plan attacks and strategize. I know these dragons far better than I know anyone else." Alitas spoke with such passion that he'd have swayed me even if I hadn't been of a similar mind. The honor guard could already be trusted, and that made them perfect.

"That just leaves you, Flick. Do you have someone in mind?"

"Jace, and then Capricia. Or maybe even both."

I lifted an eyebrow, hoping that Flick would have an explanation for me, but he only grinned and shrugged. As I thought about the strategic value of them both, I couldn't deny it would be useful. Both could command in battle, and both were dragons with other agendas that didn't match entirely with mine. Capricia had supported Grigick for the throne over me, and Jace had been exiled. When the truth came out, they would be the best proof of my willingness to give the information to whoever needed it, not just those who would unconditionally support me.

"Okay, do it. Both, if you feel up to the task."

With that settled, I pulled open my messages from the elders. Though the chambers were a short flight away, and my role involved being there a lot, they sent a constant stream of messages to me as well.

After feeling like we had a plan and I might be able to get the upper hand against this demon finally, I was instantly crestfallen when I read the messages. All the elders of the various cities had begun to respond to our call for warrior dragons to be trained and given equipment to form a global response team to the demon. So far, almost all of them were refusing to volunteer anyone. Some were refusing to even ask their dragons, insisting that it was my job to protect them, not the other way around, and that they wouldn't risk their lives for a race that didn't deserve it.

I read through each response with a heavier and heavier heart. This wasn't what our race was meant to be like. Alitas had told me each city had once had its own militia, honor guards, and dragons who trained for war and considered it an honor. It was one of the reasons I had put out the call.

I messaged the elders and asked them to continue working to get the dragon cities to understand that it wasn't a few humans in danger, but all of us. It was about protecting all of us—our friends, our children—not just humans.

As I sat back, I caught Neritas staring at me.

"We've come a long way from the day we first met," he said, as if to explain what he was thinking.

"Yet, sometimes I feel equally as clueless and overwhelmed."

"You are far stronger than you give yourself credit for. We'll find a way through this. We'll defeat this demon and lock him back up again, and we'll see peace restored. And you'll lead our nation back to greatness, with everyone treated well, free to move between cities, and with harmony between us and humanity."

"That's a lot of big tasks." I wanted to chuckle at the enormity of it.

Alitas rejoined the conversation. "A lot of them go hand in hand."

I nodded. My mind had caught on to one of the goals Neritas had mentioned: defeating the demon and locking him back up again. In some ways, they were a contradiction in terms. Surely defeating the demon would be killing him in this case? Otherwise, we would be just containing him for the next generation of dragons to worry about.

Although I didn't voice the thought out loud, I considered it for a moment. Could he be defeated? Or had my ancestors despaired of the task and settled for containment? I had no way of knowing without going to a particular island, and right now I doubted I could take time out of my tasks to run to the island of Kilnar to ask why the ancestors hadn't killed a demon thousands of years earlier.

Pushing the thought from my mind, I focused instead on my own tasks. I had a bunch of armor, weapons, and shields to activate so that more of the honor guard and the fighters who went into battle could have weaponry that didn't fail them.

In some ways, this was one of my favorite tasks. It gave me a way to protect those I cared about and help them fight back. It gave all of us a way to store power for when the enemy showed up. And that was the best thing I could do with my magic when I had no information to act on.

CHAPTER ELEVEN

As the sun set, I grew tired and had to stop activating the metals. I had grown in skill at getting them to respond and start taking energy, and I had learned where my sensible limit was, so I didn't exhaust myself for days on end. It didn't use much magic, but it did drain another part of me.

I had managed to activate another twenty items, but no full armor sets. I was still the only person wearing one of those. While there were still plenty of dragons and humans who wanted to fight but didn't have anything we could charge, it made more sense to get them all a weapon and shield than a full-body covering that I couldn't complete in less than three sessions.

With so much of me drained, I called a halt for dinner. I had been able to feel my three main companions pushing themselves as well, testing their abilities and moving magic around.

They had charged up some of the equipment I had activated on previous days. Neritas was able to draw on as many of the dragons in the city as I could. We didn't take very much magic from anyone who went into battle with us, but there were many other dragons in Detaris we could slowly draw from.

It had been something we had discussed at length in the elders' chambers publicly, letting all the dragons in Detaris weigh in on the topic. They had agreed it was okay to draw on their magic collectively, as long as we didn't cause them discomfort. While some had not been fond of the idea, wary of being drained or harmed, many had volunteered, wishing their magic to be put to good use in a fight they had no other way of joining due to age or duty.

The end result had been a promise to take no more than a certain percentage of a dragon's personal power and to leave them with enough to function in their daily tasks. For the weakest dragons, it meant taking very little, but those with something in between our level and the lowest could provide a steady stream of energy.

Since that meeting, there had also been an increase in interest in dragons strengthening themselves, training their powers, and finding a way to harness more magic for us. Given it aided us in battle, I had approved the focus and showed them once to help them get started.

Now, however, we were all hungry, and the dragons in my family and friends started to return to the tower to eat as well.

Some of them had mixed successes with their days. The military was proving difficult to deal with when they weren't talking to me directly, and everyone else was tired in one way or another. Ben didn't return, which I had expected, so I had some food sent to him in the library before I tucked in.

I was halfway through clearing my plate when Jace got a message.

"Shit. He's attacking again. Dragon city this time, but there's humans close by."

Everyone got to their feet, including me, the food forgotten. We all headed for our away bags and gear.

"Tell the elders, and get them to ask for as many volunteers as possible," I yelled as I ran to my room to get my ruck. "Then let the soldiers know if they don't already. I want us in the air as soon as possible."

"Where do we need to go?" Alitas called out as well.

"Arizona, near Phoenix," Jace called back.

I exhaled, knowing that was going to be a long fly, but not as far as Denver, at least. With any luck, we would get there in time. We had also had more warning, as the message had come from a dragon as danger approached. The city had magical defenses and plenty of us were already prepping.

Once I had everything I wanted to take, I hurried back to the main room. Alitas already had honor guards grabbing the extra weapons and shields we had activated and charged and was loading them all up with spares.

"We'll give them to any dragon who will take them when we get there," he explained.

Griffin hurried into the room. "General Miller wants to talk to you before you fly out." He was clutching a phone and must have traded numbers with the general at some point that day.

I reached out to take the phone, but he'd already hung up. I was going to have no choice but to take the meeting in person. Letting out a frustrated growl, I headed for the balcony.

"Have everyone else meet me in front of the soldier camp. I'm going to get this sorted and then fly as soon as everyone is gathered."

I didn't wait for anyone before I walked out and turned into a dragon, but Neritas, Flick, Alitas, and Reijo were already with me and forming up. Jace and several of the other honor guard weren't far behind in a second wave. Griffin didn't follow us right away but went to the elders' chambers.

Kryos went down toward Capricia and the city guard, no doubt to get some of them to come with us. Capricia wasn't one to shy away from any fight.

I sped toward the soldier camp. I must have seemed incredibly frightening when I burst out of the shield that protected Detaris and suddenly appeared in view. I pulled up hard and turned back into a human to land.

Lieutenant Douglas came rushing out and I hurried over to him.

"I believe the general is expecting me." I didn't want to waste any time.

The lieutenant nodded and motioned for me to follow him and turned before I even got to him. I slipped into a jog, wanting to get this over with quickly, and he matched my pace to see me inside the main tent. Alitas, Flick, and Neritas tried to keep up. I was pretty sure that I was pissing at least one of them off with my rush into possible danger of another kind, but they didn't voice their frustrations.

Once inside, I saw the general by his doorway holding the fabric open. I ran to him as he retreated to let us inside.

"Your elder, Griffin, informed us that this demon is attacking again." General Miller didn't go behind his desk. He stood where he was, expecting me not to waste time.

"Yes, a dragon city near Phoenix. I don't know how many humans are close, but they would be in danger as well. He won't care who else gets hurt."

"Our early intel is that your city is out in the desert and at worst we have a few hikers nearby, but no settlements or roads." The tone General Miller used immediately put me on edge. It was clear that he didn't consider this his fight.

I didn't beat around the bush. "Do you have anyone on the way to help defend?"

"The military in the area is moving to defensive positions around Phoenix and is on standby."

"Will they help?" I didn't hide the frustration from my voice as I spoke. Defensive positions were not the same as being willing to fight anyway.

"I cannot say. It's not my area of command and it's not my call." He sighed, seeming to deflate a little, and I got the impression that he'd have helped me if he could command it.

"I'd like to formally request to take some of your soldiers from here, then, General." I was torn between the waste of time this could become and wanting to rush to the defense of my own people. "I understand that some of them have fought alongside me before, at least once."

"Permission to volunteer for this mission, sir?" Lieutenant Douglas asked, not letting the general reply.

"How would my soldiers go with you? I don't have any air transport here."

"Every dragon can carry at least two soldiers."

Both officers tried to process what I was suggesting for a moment. I was offering to fly them into battle and let them ride on the backs of dragons. The general didn't look entirely convinced, but the lieutenant was enthusiastic.

"Permission to ask who else would volunteer and lead a team of volunteers, sir?" he added.

This seemed to sway General Miller. He nodded and allowed the lieutenant to rush outside the tent.

"I could order my men to stay here, but I'm no fool. There's no way I can stop the men going with you if they are as eager as they seem and not come to regret it at a later date, so I'm not going to try and stop them. Can you promise me to do everything you can to protect them and get them back here in one piece? If they come back alive, healthy, and with battle experience, I can explain this to anyone scrutinizing my decisions, but if they get hurt…"

"I understand. I'll do everything I can and protect them like I do my own kin." I meant every word, understanding that his people meant something to him, even if he'd focused more on the reaction he would get from his superiors.

My response seemed to satisfy him, because he let me leave the tent. Lieutenant Douglas and over thirty of the men and women who served in the camp came hurrying up from various parts of the camp and pledged to follow my orders as long as I could take them into battle against the demon.

It sounded as if a couple of the soldiers here were also

related to, or friends with, some who had lost their lives in the fights with the demons. They had a personal score to settle.

Whatever their reasons for volunteering, I thanked them again when we were standing without too much of an audience, and then I assigned two humans to each dragon.

"We're really going to need to hurry and get to work as soon as we get there. Can all of you handle holding onto our dragons while flying into all these things?"

"Go for it. We're used to interesting conditions. All of us in the air with you is an honor." Lieutenant Douglas tightened his bag straps so he wouldn't drop anything midflight. His whole troop followed suit.

I verified that I had enough space, and then morphed into a dragon on the ground. A lot of the others had already done the same, spreading out onto the road and into the open so we wouldn't morph around anything dangerous. One of the pieces of advice I had been given the first few times I had gone to change was not to do so among trees or in water, where anything could become trapped inside my new form.

The belongings we carried were different. They morphed with us because they were with us when we started the process, but everything else was an addition along the way. It was the biggest reason that dragon cities were built in the way they were, with tall towers and large spaces between them. In the air, we had plenty of space to transform.

When I was in dragon form and comfortable, Lieutenant Douglas and another of the soldiers he'd chosen, a sniper by the looks of his gun, came toward me.

"I apologize in advance if climbing up hurts," the lieutenant said. He was the first of all of his unit to try and get on.

You won't hurt me. My scales are tougher than anything on Earth. I said the words into the lieutenant's head and enjoyed watching his eyes go wide.

As he climbed on, I suggested the best place for him to sit and then, when he was comfortable, he helped the sniper up as well. When the two of them were sitting correctly, I gave the nod and the rest of the unit climbed onto the backs of the other dragons.

Caution was important, and I had to keep these soldiers safe, but I was desperate to get in the air again. This had taken up a lot of time and the demon would be attacking hard by now.

With more warning and a smaller distance to fly than we had to Denver, I still hoped we would get there in time.

The second the last soldier was in place and the other dragons were all in the air already, I prepared to spring up as well.

Hold on tight, I said to all of them before jumping and flapping my wings.

It was all the warning they needed, and the soldiers all kept their seats as we got into the air. I knew they would add extra weight and exhaustion to the journey, so I had already distributed them among our best fliers. A few of the dragons only had one human on their backs. It was a team that was clearly already working, however.

With Alitas leading the way again, I encouraged the

group to fly as fast and as hard as they could for our city in Arizona. It was imperative we got there before anyone got hurt.

We might not be able to do much. The demon was ruthless and would use large forces, and cities could only be defended for so long, even the ones designed to stand against him.

As we flew, I tried not to think about what I might find beyond strategic planning for all eventualities. Most of them resulted in the same response, however. Attack hard and fast and get into a defensive position around the city. And get Kryos and his team on the ground to hand out weapons and shields to whoever had the power left to defend their home.

It wasn't a perfect strategy, but Alitas hadn't seen this city in many years and he hadn't been the captain of the honor guard at the time. We had no idea what we would find.

All we could do was fly hard.

CHAPTER TWELVE

It took a couple of hours of intense flying to get to the point where we could see something on the horizon. A minute or so later, I felt the demons with my mind, a mass presence of shadow catchers, handlers, the great demon himself, and all of the strange creatures he had begun to enslave.

There's a lot of unfriendlies, I told everyone. *And they've got the city encircled. We need to punch through and form a defense around them if we can. And there's a good chance that the demon is going to come straight for me.*

He won't reach you, Alitas replied, and I heard the anger in his voice. This was going to be a fierce battle and the demon wasn't going to know what hit him.

This close, I reached for whatever I could charge that hadn't been charged already, feeling forward for the city and its defense line as well. There were dragons out there and they were trying to use their magic, but the city was overrun.

Roaring my frustration to buy them more time as well

as give them hope, I made it known that we had arrived. Immediately the demonic army reacted, and the demon in the sky reeled about to face us.

"He looks pissed off," Lieutenant Douglas yelled so I could hear him. He wasn't wrong, but if the demon was angry right now, he was going to be even more angry in a few minutes.

Some demons on the ground and their handlers also turned to face us, but the majority continued to focus on the city. Whatever he had come here for, he didn't have it yet. That gave me hope. I might have gotten here too late to stop there being any loss of life, but I had gotten here before he had won.

I flew directly for the demon and charged the scales of every single dragon in the air as well as the soldiers themselves. Some of them were holding the spare shields we had, and I felt Lieutenant Douglas shift his to bring it up in front of him.

I made a mental note to look into getting a harness with a shield built into it so, if this sort of fight ever happened again, a human could crouch and shoot from behind it. With the right charged weapons, it could make this demon think twice about ever doing anything but running and hiding.

For now, however, we would have to fight as best we could with what we had. And if nothing else, I had anger fueling my actions.

The demon flew toward us, but he didn't come alone. All the strange, corrupted birds the people in Denver had described were with him.

Can you kill most of these and thin them out? I asked the

soldiers, knowing they would drain our charges without doing much damage. They were cannon fodder, and I wanted them gone with the least amount of energy expended on our part.

"We'll do our best," Lieutenant Douglas replied as they opened fire. I tried to think of the best way to kill as many of them as possible as fast as possible.

The soldiers opened fire. They were all good shots, and their targets were relatively easy to hit when flying directly toward us as we were flying at them. Within a few seconds, almost a hundred fell from the sky, but there were so many of them it barely did anything more than thin the herd.

I roared again, noticing that the demon had held back and let the birds overtake him. He was trying to slow us down.

Leave those birds to me and anyone not with a soldier on their back. I've got an idea. Can you keep our scales charged, though? Jace asked.

Of course, I replied before getting the soldiers to stop and every dragon who carried them to lift up above the creatures. I was going to see this through and break through to the city, and I was determined that we would all have enough charge when we got there.

Drawing hard on the connection I had with the isle of the ancestors, I also pulled magic from all of the dragons and pumped it into charging Jace's groups scales, as she had asked.

As Jace formed up her second group below me, the soldiers continued to take any shots they thought would benefit us most.

Leave the demon to your honor guard second unit, Alitas

told just me. *Head for the city and do what you do best. Rally the troops and get them working together.*

I didn't like the idea of leaving them to face someone who could kill them all easily, but now that Alitas knew how to move magic, they would fare better than I feared. And he was right. I could do more to help us by getting to the city.

Once again, our group split. Alitas led his group of honor guards and soldiers as I flew hard toward the city over the top of all of them.

The demon made to come at me regardless, but Alitas also had Jared with him, and that dragon could *fly*. He got in the way at every turn, and I pumped more magic into him to help him move faster as I passed.

Despite attacking our approach, the majority of the forces the demon commanded were still attacking the city. It was on water, for the most part, so there weren't as many ways in to attack, but the demons had collapsed some of the buildings and created walkways. The handlers were clearly in control and smarter than the shadow catchers.

I flew down over the top of them with nothing to stop me anymore, and the soldiers shot at the shadow catchers and handlers that had gotten into the civilized area.

The dragons in the city were in human form and had at least developed a defense strategy. They were using long objects such as curtain poles and broom handles to knock shadow catchers into the water. For the most part, it was helping, but the shadow catchers were decaying the objects and making them shorter, until the dragons had to retreat or find something else.

Some shadow catchers that fell in the water weren't

dying, either. The water was too shallow in some places to overload them before they could get out and clear. They were getting back up again quickly and were then more powerful, having had a good soak of their life-enhancing liquid. And all of them were drawing on the mass of water to supercharge themselves.

After so long fighting them on drier terrain, I had forgotten how much harder they were when near water and able to draw it to them.

I targeted the nearest set of shadow catchers, flying by and using my dragon limbs to knock them back into the water for now and buy us some relief if any did explode. I needed to find somewhere to land and drop my soldiers, but to do that I had to push back the demons near the city.

As the dragons with me attempted to do the same, I realized that it wasn't going to work. Flick, Neritas, and a couple of the honor guards could fly that well, but even Capricia wasn't used to this city and couldn't do much. And it used a lot of charge on the dragons to knock off the demons while we were in dragon form.

Coming around again, satisfied that I'd at least saved a few lives and taken the pressure off where I could, I looked for somewhere we could land.

Land in the water, Flick suggested. *Just deep enough we have some distance between us and danger and then fight over to the city.*

It was the closest thing to a decent plan. I considered a pincer movement, having half our remaining group land on the other side of the city and shoreline, but we were a small enough group already. We needed to punch through and fight across, arming the dragons as we did.

I swooped down, letting the soldiers know they were going to be dropped a few feet. I transformed, and they fell. I landed in front of them, pulled the shield off my back, and charged the shore right in front of me as well as the edge of the city beside me. We pushed back and killed several shadow catchers as the soldiers opened fire and more dragons landed and unloaded as well.

The dragons formed a wall in front of the soldiers without shields to protect them.

I got everyone together and surveyed the area as shadow catchers tried to rush us but hit the wall of charged water and brick. It made them screech, but I was getting used to the noise.

The demons were still flooding into the city in the center, probably trying to make a route toward the artifact the demon was after.

It gave me a goal: to fight over there and stop them while saving as many dragons as I could on the way. I started pushing, recharging the area in front of me enough to get to the shore. I reached it and stopped draining the magic, then used the sword and shield to push and attack, hitting the shadow catchers hard. With Neritas on one side of me and Flick on the other, we pushed them back. The three of us were an efficient team.

Soldiers had slotted into our fighting wall on either side of them, and Capricia and Kryos had the line. We formed a wedge with me at the front, as I turned across the shoreline and tried to move. I didn't focus on killing the demons so much as getting myself in position to defend the city.

The handlers saw the threat we presented, and several of them started coming our way. There were two of the many-tentacled kind and another that almost looked as if it was some kind of large tree, with branches and vines whipping out.

These three alone were going to grind our progress to a halt.

Thinking fast, I searched for a better way to get to where I wanted to be. We couldn't save the city if we never got there.

"Neritas, you're with me. Flick, hold the group. You're in charge. Get the city dragons armed."

"You can't handle three of those, just the two of you." Flick took my arm to stop me.

I didn't know if he was wrong or right, but I didn't want to take too many from the group and stop them from being as successful. We had to save the dragons in the city as well as fight off anything that came at us.

When I looked at the sheer numbers this demon had in his army, I knew this was a fool's errand. We could hold out for hours against this kind of force, and with all the charged magical items I had, I thought we might end up winning as well, but not if we kept splitting up. We had to protect more and more dragons. I needed fighters.

"Let me come with you, me and my two best shooters," Lieutenant Douglas shouted above the noise. I was going to need to protect them as well, and I got the impression that Flick wasn't going to leave my side either.

"I've got this group. Go cut the head off the controllers and buy us some confusion," Capricia replied.

It was the enthusiasm I needed to hear. With everyone agreed on a strategy, I speared forward, heading straight for the nearest handler as Neritas and Flick shifted to the sides and let the two sharpest shooters slot in behind us. Lieutenant Douglas brought up the rear. Taking a small blade from Flick that he could thrust with, he abandoned his gun in favor of close-quarters fighting.

The two soldiers, protected in a square of warriors, took shots over my shoulders at the two handlers, hitting them with charged bullets before they got to us. It slowed them, buying me time to end the existence of a few more shadow catchers and charge the path for Capricia and her dragons to get toward the front of the city where the majority of the shadow catchers were attacking.

I glanced up a couple of times to see Alitas keeping the demon in the sky busy while Jace led the group that had almost entirely taken care of the birds. It was hard to keep track of all the items and dragons that needed recharging when juggling this many, but Neritas and Flick had Jace covered and Alitas was managing his small squad on his own.

I needed more to help me, but knowing that we were training them now and they would soon be able to do it gave me some comfort.

The handlers kept coming closer and the tentacles were soon near enough to whip over our heads. I stopped us where we were and shifted into a tighter group, to protect the soldiers.

It wasn't easy having to brace against the tentacle attacks, but every time they whipped at our shields and my armor, it hurt them too, and the charge on our metals didn't run out in the same way it did on basic metals. Each impact hurt, however.

With the third swipe from a tentacle, Neritas and I

managed to hack in toward each other on either side and almost entirely lop it off. At the same time, Flick stepped out of formation and shoved another to the side before chopping it off with a single down stroke.

A shadow catcher tried to dive through the gap Flick had left, but the lieutenant shifted and blocked. The soldier shot it as Flick came back and pushed it away with his shield.

I reached into a small pouch, grabbed my disks, and flung them back toward it, finishing the catcher off and buying time for Flick to get fully back.

Neritas caught the next flail, and I stabbed upward underneath it, cutting out another chunk of rotten flesh. No sooner had we rebuffed it than a loud screeching roar came from the sky.

I looked up toward the demon flying up there, hoping to see that he was hurt or struggling, but he seemed to power up and away from Alitas. He rushed toward the city as the flow of shadow catchers and handlers changed. Instead of rushing in, some were now rushing out with a handler in their midst.

"They've got the artifact," I said, hoping to change direction, but there was nothing I could do. Even if I launched into the air and let the soldiers die, I was too far away to get there in time.

Instead, I pulled magic from every source I could find and tried to charge a wall of air between the city and the handler who must be holding it. I gave everything else I could to Alitas, lending him the speed of all the dragons in the air. He was the closest and the most skilled fighter we had.

The handler closest to me didn't give up, lashing out at me and the others as the second one reached us. I had no choice but to defend us and attack the handlers. I had no doubt now that these three were a sacrifice to keep me busy.

They were going to pay, regardless. Knowing this battle was going to come to an end soon, one way or another, I charged the ground around us.

It pushed back and killed all the shadow catchers nearby, allowing us to fall out of formation and protect the soldiers in a different way from the flailing tentacles and vines.

With more freedom to move, I could sever the limbs and fight back more effectively. Douglas grabbed the flying disks I'd thrown from where they hung in the air and looked at them.

"Fling them at the enemies and they'll electrocute them," I explained. It wasn't a perfect example of what would happen, but it was close enough.

He didn't need any more encouragement and got straight to work, using them to help fight back against the handlers.

I powered us forward, keeping the area charged so all the soldiers could shoot and let us stab out from the safe zone I'd created.

When the charged area reached the handler, it tried to fall back, but one of its tentacles flailed, and instead of chopping it off I pushed it down to the ground with my shield and stamped on it. Neritas stabbed down with his blade, driving it downward with so much force that it impaled the tentacle into the ground.

The handler wriggled and yanked, screaming in pain, but it couldn't move without severing its own limb. It allowed us to flow out and around it as I charged the ground, leaving it writhing in pain while I ran to attack the next.

Fighting without thought and trying to take out as many of the controlling handlers as I could, I sucked magic from every non-dragon source. At the same time, I tried to keep the barrier up, keeping the demon away from the handler that was trying to get out of the city.

Alitas had reached the demon, my barrier having slowed him, but the demon seemed to entirely ignore the captain of the honor guard and continued trying to find a way toward his minion.

As I drove my sword deep into the heart of a handler and made the majority of its body dissipate into smoke, the demon punched a hole through my wall and almost fell upon the handler with the artifact.

The demon let out a shriek and all the minions rushed toward him, many of them turning from combat they were in the middle of.

He grabbed the handler and the artifact it carried and flew away with them.

Most of the shadow catchers and handlers tried to follow, as if the fight had gone out of them and they knew they shouldn't be carrying on. All of them tried to run away, though that was a stupid decision for them.

I took advantage, killing everything in reach and regrouping with my kind.

CHAPTER THIRTEEN

Exhausted, and aware of the complete devastation of the city, I walked toward it. There were still a few shadow catchers here and there, but they were all trying to flee, outnumbered and very easy prey for my fighters to pick off.

We had failed. The demon had left with the artifact part he wanted. I could have sworn, or grown very angry at someone, or all manner of other things. Instead, I was too tired to make much of a fuss.

After rushing the great distance to get here, I'd known we were going to arrive too late to help everyone, but I had truly hoped that we would be able to save the artifact and fight him off.

Instead, we had only delayed him from getting what he wanted.

Despite how angry I was at myself, I gathered all the soldiers and dragons to me. It had been an intense battle, but no one was seriously hurt and only a few wounds were bad enough to need some kind of medical assistance.

I pulled out the healing device and got to work, doing what I could while the rest of the folks I cared for joined us. It wasn't long before I was healing citizens of the city as well, brought to me by relatives or whoever cared enough.

Without complaint or sign of tiredness, I healed them as well. It struck me as almost ironic, because this city had been one of the dragon cities that didn't want to send anyone to help me in the fights against the dragon and his scum.

It made me want to turn away the dragons coming to me now. If they weren't willing to protect the world with me, then it was rich of them to have me defend their city or heal their wounds. And this was without the problems I'd had the time before that, before I'd been crowned.

When I had healed about two-thirds of the dragons in front of me, a very injured one was brought out on a stretcher borne by several older and more ornately dressed dragons.

"Your Highness, we beg you to consider our plea and help to heal those of us who have been hurt by this attack."

I looked over the wounded dragon, a strong-looking young man who had several decay marks on him. To have taken so many hits across his body, he must have been defending something or someone.

No matter how I'd have been asked, I would have healed a person so obviously willing to be brave and face danger, and I quickly ran the healing device over him, starting with his torso and what appeared to be the worst of the wounds.

It took a long time to heal him, and Neritas came to help me before it was done. The dragon never woke up, but he looked like he was resting easier when I was finished.

While I and the other dragons with healing devices tended to as many wounded as we could, Alitas, Lieutenant Douglas, and Capricia worked together to get the city safe and everyone sheltered for now.

I tried not to think about failing, or how many of the enemy had gotten away. Facing the demon like this made it abundantly clear that I didn't have enough fighters or enough magic, and I wouldn't know where I needed to be soon enough.

By the time I had healed everyone, there was very little magic left in all the dragons near me, including myself, and I had used a good portion of the magic in the armor and all the chargeable equipment as well. I couldn't handle another fight like this any time soon.

That had me more worried, but I didn't dare pull magic from any more dragons. The injured needed rest, and those who had come out of the fight physically unscathed were bearing other sorts of burdens. This had been a city that hadn't seen anything detrimental for a very long time.

The elders were all gathered under the shade of an army awning. I'd seen one of the soldiers pull it from his bag and tie it to four sticks, then he and his companions spread it out and staked it into the ground. It provided shelter from the sun and allowed Alitas to talk to them.

"Scarlet, you might want to hear what they have to say," he said when he saw me. "And eat and drink something while you listen."

Neritas and Flick weren't far behind me, so when I was offered a plate of food I insisted that they be taken care of as well. Without standing on ceremony, I plonked myself down on the ground.

The dirt underneath me made a squelchy sound and I realized I'd just made my ass filthy, but it was a secondary concern. My clothes were still damp after landing in the water to fight, and my footwear was still drenched.

"What did he take?" I asked in between mouthfuls of food. I was so hungry that I continued to shovel in the creamy mashed potatoes and fried chicken I'd been handed while I waited for someone to explain.

"We don't know exactly what it was. It was in an old storage area in the city that we haven't been to in some time. It was locked and well-guarded. Our records of it were either destroyed or lost over time," one of the elders to my right offered. He was a mouse-like gentleman with spectacles on his nose.

"Describe it, if you can."

"It was a… rod, I guess. Just a—"

"Stick," a new dragon said as he came walking up. "Looked like it was a fancy stick. The first big demon that tried to take it got a nasty shock. Practically melted into a pile of goo before my eyes." He sat as well, also not seeming to care about the dirt.

"Thanks," I replied. "I'm Scarlet."

"I gathered. I'm Jeff and I'd like to volunteer to fight."

"I appreciate that, Jeff. But I need to have a word with your elders before I consider volunteers. You see, I messaged them only half a day ago, asking if anyone in their city would join the fight against the demons and start training so we had more dragons all over the place able to hold the fort until I could fly to the scene of every attack and help. Do you know what they replied to me?"

Jeff looked up and around the dragons under the makeshift awning. The elders all had the good grace to look away as if they now regretted their response.

"Let me guess. They thought it best if we didn't get involved."

"Something like that. I'll spare you the exact details, but I didn't get any enthusiasm or any fighters to train here or equip for any possible battles."

"Well, I don't answer to them. I'll fight."

I squeezed his shoulder. Although I appreciated the sentiment, it was one person, and it didn't solve my bigger issue. If we had any chance of stopping this demon, I needed the elders of each city to understand the danger they were in. Maybe, now that one of our cities had been attacked and decimated, they would stop being so cautious and actually sign up.

"Reijo, can you take pictures of the destruction here, the injured and the dead, and see that they're sent to the elders of all the dragon cities, please?" I finished eating and got up, handing my plate to someone else. Reijo nodded and hurried off.

The elders all looked up and stopped shuffling their feet.

"We're very sorry. If we—"

I lifted my hand and shook my head, cutting the elder off from making a very lame excuse and giving me the worst explanation for what was simply cowardice.

"I expect all of you to explain to *your* people why you didn't get help any sooner and issue them a formal apology. I want you to let them know that you neglected to ask them if they'd volunteer, despite my requesting it and making the threat to our race abundantly clear. They deserve to know what happened and then be asked the question you should have asked them in the first place: Who wants to fight and be equipped to defend their home should the worst happen?"

Although I was polite and kept my tone even, so much anger and indignation rose up inside me as I spoke that I could barely contain it.

The elders nodded, none of them daring to speak.

Without another word, I walked away. If I stayed, I knew that I would be so angry I'd lash out. It wasn't all the elders' fault, however. I felt angry because they were attacked and hurt, and I hadn't known they were going to be the next target. I was angry because not only had my own race rejected my appeal for volunteers, but I also didn't get any help from the humans of the planet either, other than a few soldiers.

There were lots of reasons to be angry. The hard part was channeling that anger into something that would make a difference.

I had to get ahead of this problem. As I looked over all the dragons under my command, I considered them. The exhausted ones who had flown all this way with me, fought with everything they had, given all their magic, and were still on their feet trying to take care of the dragons from this city.

On top of that, I now had the hurt, sick, and unsheltered dragons from the city. While the weather wasn't too bad at this time of year, it wasn't great either. I needed to get them a place to stay until the city could be repaired and strengthened again.

The weaponry and armor my team had handed out during the fight also seemed woefully inadequate. More dragons here needed weapons, and this was just one of many cities.

Scale was my biggest problem. I had the dragons. They simply didn't have the understanding, the gear, or the experience, all because one of my ancestors had once decided that no one needed to know that the gate needed recharging. Instead, he'd spread the word that the demon was dealt with forever.

As I thought about this, I realized I needed to do something before I got some sleep or went back to Detaris.

"I'd like to go to Kilnar." I didn't care who heard me. "I want to go as soon as possible."

"Are you sure you can get us there?" Flick asked.

I knew he was trying to get me to consider it sensibly. I didn't have Ben or my mother with me, and it would be the first time I would have to try to get there without either of them. On both previous occasions, my mother had navigated the tricky waters for us. This time I didn't plan on taking so long either.

"We'll fly the whole way there." It was the only explanation I wanted to give, and I wasn't going to take no for an answer.

After flying here, going north to Kilnar and then having to fly back to Detaris was going to be a long journey. We were going to need a bunch of supplies and a moment to recharge before we left. And I was going to have to be sure of the people we carried as well.

I called Alitas over and considered my options and what I needed. He helped me make a plan, especially considering that I needed to keep things in motion and people well-fed. On top of that, I had to make sure someone could reach us at any time. The last thing I wanted was for there to be another attack and for no help to arrive at all, even if I arrived late.

We opted to leave a few dragons behind. The city needed guidance and training, and they could return to Detaris in due time. In their place, I took a few of this city's rookies who were desperate to help. It wasn't a perfectly fair trade. I was leaving experienced dragons and taking those who hadn't seen any combat before the last few hours.

The dragons I was leaving behind were better suited to help, but I was confident it wouldn't be long before they joined me. Then I'd have an even bigger army.

It was dark by the time we were ready to leave, and the elders were trying to persuade me to stay. There was nowhere for me or any of the dragons with me to sleep, however, and I wasn't going to waste any more time that would give the demon a chance to regroup and attack the next place.

If the ancestors had any information that might help, I wanted it as soon as was physically possible.

We got in the air by the time the moon was out. All of us were carrying the soldiers. I appreciated that it was harder on them than the rest of us, and we flew a little slower, but I still followed the connection I had to the ancestors, feeling it grow stronger and the magic I could pull from it go up as I got closer.

I drew from the connection, gently feeding it to everyone with me and helping us all to keep flying and stay awake. As we got closer, I drew more, hoping to charge as much equipment as possible again. Given that the demon was attacking so often, I would have very little chance to recharge everything to fight again.

As we flew, I watched the lights of human cities come and go underneath us, slipping by in a haze of need and tiredness.

No one spoke, but I had the familiar comfort of Flick and Neritas on each side of me, with Alitas below. I led the way this time, the only one sure of the direction because no one else could fully sense it.

We flew over the lake and briefly landed on the shore to have drinks and give our passengers a moment to stretch their legs, take a toilet break, and see if they needed anything from the supplies.

Every dragon remained in dragon form. We could keep going, and I was very eager to go to the island and talk to my ancestors.

When the soldiers were ready again, we took to the skies. I held low this time, near the water, but still high enough that we didn't disturb any wildlife below us. It was time to talk to my ancestors.

CHAPTER FOURTEEN

When we passed through the barrier that kept the isle of Kilnar hidden, the lieutenant gasped. Even in the dark, it had an outline, and it appeared as if by magic.

I didn't explain how it had suddenly appeared, but stayed silent as I followed the tugging thread deep inside me and the connection I had with the ancestors. We were safe here, as long as we didn't take a wrong path, and by flying this way we would bypass almost all of those.

Heading straight for the plateau near the top, I led everyone to the resting spot and landed. The soldiers hopped off, we turned into human form, and most of the dragons went about making a camp for everyone. It was the third or fourth time some of them had been there, and they all knew where to find supplies and what was and wasn't okay on the island.

It allowed me to focus on the reason I was there—to go see my ancestors.

Without my mom there to guide me, it felt a little strange, but Neritas and Flick went with me so I wasn't alone. Although Alitas looked as if he wished to join me, he knew I would come to no harm and that this connection was something special and important to me.

I made the climb with my two closest friends and tried not to think beyond asking the ancestors for advice. They had once refused to respond, when I had brought Grigick here. When he had tried to commune with them and gain their approval, they had simply refused to connect.

Despite having their favor so far, I always feared that they would reject me too. I wasn't good enough to be queen, in my mind, and I never would be. But there weren't a lot of options. My mother and Grigick were the only other red dragons we could find. Although, of course, now I had discovered that the color of our scales didn't really matter.

Any powerful dragon might be a better leader than I was.

The pathway was as beautiful as ever, the plants on either side glowed slightly and lit our way as if they were there just for us and responding to our presence. It was stunning and made me feel calmer.

At the top, the usual pedestal waited in the middle of a circle, with several other spots around it ready for key people in my life. Neritas and Flick stood in the places my mom and Ben usually took.

I considered telling them to back away and leave it to me, in case this wasn't what we were meant to do, but I felt a strange calmness as I neared the pedestal in the center, almost as if this was exactly what we should be doing. I trusted my gut and let them stay where they were.

As I put my hands on the pedestal, I felt the connection

I had with the island strengthen. A second later, it was as if I was sucked into an imaginary place in my head. I was suddenly standing in the middle of a large field, alone and scared for a few seconds.

Normally when I appeared in these, I could sense the ancestors right away, but not this time. I was simply alone.

I looked around, trying to work out if I had done something wrong, or if I was dreaming, or if I'd broken the connection somehow. Eventually, a figure seemed to step out of the shadows. He smiled, a little taller than me and with the same shade of hair as me, although his was spiked up all over his head as if he had been running his hands through it. I recognized him, but at the same time didn't. This wasn't my father, but he looked a lot like him.

"Hello, Scarlet. I'm sorry I've not come to talk to you before now. It's not always easy to get this right."

Not sure how to respond to this, I stayed silent, which made him chuckle.

"This is the third time you have come before us. What is it you need?"

"Advice, and information that seems to have been lost to the ages. Items that were put safe and forgotten about and are now needed again." It wasn't a full description, but I studied him as I spoke. He nodded as if he knew exactly what I was talking about.

"The artifacts," he said.

I nodded.

"We separated them to keep everyone safe. They could funnel extreme amounts of power and draw from...less than usual sources. If they had remained lying around as they were, they could have been used to do great harm—

drain a single dragon entirely dry or attack a city. Many things."

Although I had suspected something like this as an explanation, I didn't like it.

"I need them." It was a simple statement, and I meant to say it with force and conviction that showed I was in command and expecting this ghost I had summoned to obey me. Instead, it came out as more of a plea. If he didn't help, I didn't know what I'd do.

"Not all the ancestors agree that you should be helped."

"That's not my problem right now. If they want to sit in judgment, then they can go ahead. But they're not on Earth, walking this walk, and they're not making the decisions. I'm trying to save the planet. I might not get every part in this puzzle exactly right, but I try."

"And that's why I'm here. I insisted on being allowed to help you."

The relief I felt was immediate. I hadn't come all this way for nothing. But it didn't sound as if I was going to get everything I needed either.

"What can you tell me?" I asked after a few seconds of him not saying anything.

"When I was in your position there was a sort of rhyme…a ditty, if you like."

I waited for him to continue and elaborate on his own.

"The rhyme is lost to time and memory. I don't remember most of it, but you'll find it somewhere you've looked once before and haven't looked recently."

This was not helpful, and my face probably showed my dissatisfaction at being fed such vague advice.

After a few seconds, the man in front of me chuckled.

"I've always wanted to do that. Give some kind of vague prophecy and see how someone reacted."

"Well, it's less than awesome when people are dying out here. So what have I forgotten, missed, or need to go take a look at?"

"Your mentor, Anthony. He was a good dragon, and he knew a lot more than he could ever get to tell you. His journal is in your hands. It's worth translating the rest."

"But we never figured out any more key phrases. We tried everything we could think of." I shrugged, knowing that this conversation was happening in my head and wondering if it was partially my subconscious having it with itself. Was this a way to access another part of my brain that already knew all these things?

The guy opposite me frowned, making me wonder if he could read my mind.

"Are you going to keep being vague, or are there phrases you can tell me as well?" I asked. After the day I had survived and how long I had been awake, I really wasn't in the mood for games.

"You've tried them all before, just not for a while. I think. To be honest, I lost track, but you should try some of the phrases that didn't work before on later pages. Even if you don't get everything in there, you'll get more."

"And this is the great help I'm getting from the all-powerful ancestors?" I crossed my arms. I was certain I looked more pissed off than I actually was.

He chuckled again, seeing through my mock displeasure. Without a word, he came closer to me and took my hands, uncrossing my arms. I was surprised to be able to feel his skin, warm against mine. There were several scars on his hands, wrists, and lower arms, much in the same way my mother's skin was scarred. He'd fought the demons as well. Had he died fighting?

I met his gaze, truly looking at him for the first time. Understanding dawned on me. This was another relation of mine.

For a second I couldn't speak, my mouth falling open as I tried to process what was happening. While I had communed with the ancestors before, it had been different each time. Although I had met my father before, this was still someone who cared for me for some reason.

"I'm your grandfather," he said as if he could read my mind. "You've grown into a young woman I am immensely proud of, Scarlet. Your path isn't and hasn't been smooth, and I hope you can forgive me for the part I played in your early life and its difficulties. Neither I nor your father were there for you, but you're right, there is more we can do now, and I fear you're going to need it."

He smiled as he let go of my hands and stepped back.

"You've got this, kiddo."

I couldn't speak, but I also didn't try to hide the tears that had overflowed from my eyes and made tracks down my cheeks. This was my grandfather, and although I didn't know exactly what part he had played in me being left in an orphanage, I knew it hadn't been unknown to him, and neither had he been uninvolved.

My mother had told me more of my father's plans. Enough to understand them even if I didn't like them or agree with them. She had barely spoken of my grandfather, her father-in-law.

Despite everything that had happened, I didn't feel

ready or prepared for the life I was meant to lead. I felt adrift and in need of a parental figure. But as quickly as he appeared, he was gone.

Once more, I was standing on top of a mountain with nothing in front of me but a pedestal. I reached for it to connect again, but I felt a difference compared to before. There was no one there to connect to. Not right now.

The difference in my connection to the island itself was also obvious. It was stronger and growing larger, with a more powerful energy behind it. I stayed where I was a little longer, not speaking despite Neritas and Flick staring at me with a thousand questions in their eyes.

I was connected to a far more powerful source than before, and I experimented with how much magic I could draw from it, funneling some of it into the sword, shield, and armor I carried.

If there had been no other gain from coming to the isle of Kilnar, this was a big one. With a magic supply like this, I might never run out again. I would always be able to hold my own in a fight. It wouldn't stretch to a large army, but it would give me the ability to store magic and put up more of a fight.

My trip here had been worth it. I could take what I had gained here back to Detaris. The journals were all safe, sitting in the tower room I called my own now. After I'd become queen and the dragon behind the gate became my entire focus, I hadn't thought it could really tell me anything new.

It seemed that I was wrong. Very wrong.

Finally, I stepped out of the circle and moved to Flick

and Neritas. The latter lifted a finger and wiped the tears off my cheek and chin, his gaze questioning still.

"I'm okay," I replied. "I met with my grandfather this time. He's given me more power and made my connection to the island stronger. Might have a lead on the location of the rest of those artifacts as well."

Although I was as open as I dared to be about what had happened, I still felt as if the meeting had been private on some level. I didn't want to talk about the details they didn't need.

Thankfully, Flick and Neritas respected my privacy and didn't ask about the rest. They simply walked with me back down the mountain.

"I can feel the extra magic coming out of the place for you. It feels…different." Neritas was the first to speak when we were about halfway back to the others.

"Don't think it's something we can connect to, though," Flick added. "I can see the connection is there for you and feel the magic and power flowing toward you. But it's not something I can tap into."

"Me neither. It's like it's off-limits. It has a sort of marker on it that makes it yours only."

I took this information in. It hadn't occurred to me that one of them might be able to tap into the same source. In some ways, I was grateful they couldn't. It was a strong indicator that I was meant to have it and not anyone else. That I had the support of the ancestors and, for some reason, they had chosen me to lead our people.

Not that I felt any better about what I was doing, or if I was more likely to succeed on my own. I had more magic. That was enough.

When we got to the camp again, the sky was beginning to brighten, and everyone had rested and eaten. Alitas came straight up to me.

"Are you okay?" he asked. "The island feels stranger."

"It does. But it's a good thing. For now." I took the offering of a roll and some hot soup and sat by one of the small campfires while everyone else woke up.

Lieutenant Douglas was one of the first to appear, and he came straight over to me.

"This place is truly extraordinary. Even I can feel the power that runs through the ground and fills the air and plants here. And all of us saw the brilliant flash of light a few hours ago that came with that increase of power." He sat opposite me and took his own mug of soup.

"The ancestors gave me more power to help in the fight." I wasn't sure how much I should say, but the lieutenant nodded.

"I can see why you'd get more of that. You're fighting for all of us and doing the part of many soldiers. That's no easy task."

"It's not. But it has fallen to me, and someone has to try and stop this demon." I shrugged and focused on eating for a while. We continued to consume our food until the majority of the camp was ready to go again and the supplies had been packed up.

It was time to return to Detaris and resupply, find out what the others had learned, and then head out again to train and retrieve artifacts before the demon did.

CHAPTER FIFTEEN

With the two soldiers flying on my back, I tried to avoid pushing myself too hard or riding through any major weather system. While I could withstand many things in my dragon form, they weren't able to, and I didn't want to make them sick.

No one had reported seeing the demon anywhere since I had last fought him, but I didn't doubt that he was lurking out there somewhere and I would need to deal with him soon.

I talked a little to the two soldiers, explaining to them some differences between our races and making it clear that we were on Earth to protect humanity, and that dragons wanted two things: to live happily ever after in their own little castle and to protect Earth from the enemy.

Lieutenant Douglas asked me several questions about the gate, how it had broken, and what we had been trying to do to fix it. During the whole conversation, he kept a very nonjudgmental tone and made me feel as if he was only trying to learn.

The sniper with him was more quiet but no less interested in knowing how to be an effective weapon against the enemy. I was grateful that they saw every fight with the demons as important and necessary to defend humanity as well as us. I noticed that no other humans but the soldiers Douglas commanded had helped us defend the last city.

If we didn't find a way to be allies in every battle, this wasn't going to work. With the US Army supporting me and more dragons, we might stand a chance of stopping the demon. Fragmented and cowering, we would all die.

It still felt strange to fly over so many locations. Until recently, this had been forbidden. We didn't land, however, and we kept fairly high up in the air so that no one could see us easily. We couldn't spot anyone stopping to look at us either.

By the time the area around Detaris was in sight, I was beyond tired. I had been up all night and I'd spent the day before fighting. Magical energy-wise, I felt really good, having been able to draw slowly on the link to the ancestors. I'd sent some of that to Neritas and Flick as well to help the pair recover.

I wasn't drawing on the magic so much at the moment, taking a little to trickle it into the items everyone was carrying on the backs of the dragons around me. It would all help in battle, and I knew that the soldiers we carried with us had earned our trust and respect. The shields and swords we had given them were theirs to keep.

The army camp that had started out as a tent with more room for press interviews than anything was becoming something more permanent. In the twenty-four hours or so that I had been gone, they'd added toilets and other small constructions. Trees had been chopped down in an area behind the tent, clearing the ground for further construction.

Although I saw the usefulness of having an ally's military power so close to us in some ways, it also made me feel threatened and worried. This could go either way, even though it was going well so far and the general in charge was helping me far more than hindering.

I was eager to get back to Detaris, but I didn't head straight there. I sent anyone who didn't have a soldier with them back to the city to rest and let the elders know what had happened, although I didn't doubt that they would have heard already. The rest of us landed by the road, easing down and letting the soldiers dismount.

They formed up with the lieutenant as the rest of us morphed back into human form. By the time everyone was standing around and changed, the general had appeared.

"Is everyone all right?" he asked, looking over all of us.

I appreciated the sentiment and was quick to nod to reassure him. "A few injuries, but minor, and I've used one of our devices to heal them up as much as possible. I can come back in a few hours, or send another dragon with the skill to help progress the healing even further. They'll all be fit for duty again by tomorrow."

His eyes widened as I spoke, as if the very thought of getting them back on their feet so fast was the craziest thing he'd ever heard. It reminded me that I had a lot of benefits as a dragon, and that they were benefits the human world didn't have. I was better as an ally than an enemy.

"Permission to dismiss the troops and debrief, sir?" Douglas asked as he came up to the general.

"Okay, get them to give back the toys and, if you're willing to stay, Your Highness, I'd appreciate hearing how the battle went from your mouth as well. It would make my report easier if I can say I'm satisfied you had everything under control."

Although I wanted to say no and rest, I nodded. I motioned to Flick and Neritas to stand down. I would be fine without them.

"They don't need to give back the kit," I replied. "They earned it, and it will help them help us in the future. I'll just need to recharge it after major battles."

The general raised his eyebrows, but he motioned for me and the lieutenant to follow him into the tent. This time, his office had some extra layers of fabric around it. When the door flap swished shut behind us, it became a lot quieter inside. He'd had it soundproofed a little, something I had no doubt would be very useful.

For the most part, I let the lieutenant tell General Miller what had happened. I only jumped in to fill in details that I needed to explain, such as why we had landed in the water and what I'd done to keep everyone safe.

"My sources say that you didn't fly straight back here. The battle ended a long time ago now." The general sat back in his chair and folded his arms across his chest.

"We were getting to that. Her highness took us to her sanctuary of sorts where she gained more power and we rested for the night in complete safety." Douglas spoke as if it had been nothing, a simple trip.

"The island of my ancestors," I added, knowing this

would need some more explaining, but not wanting to give up everything. "I needed to make the detour to get some information and aid, and I knew the lieutenant and his men would be safe there."

"And how am I meant to explain this to my superiors in Washington?" he asked.

"Don't. We stopped off at a safe place off to one side of the route back so the dragons could be rested enough to continue protecting us. Everyone has already sworn that it will be all we'll say on the matter going forward. We've only told you more out of courtesy and respect as our leader and for letting us go in the first place. I know you could command us to tell you now, but with all due respect, General, we volunteered for this and we'd like to know that you've got our back when we've been rewarded for our aid in a way that we want to keep to ourselves. We were trusted by her highness and her dragons and we'd like to keep that trust."

The general glanced at me, and I shrugged again. I had no idea that they'd talked about it and had assumed that I would have to explain the location away.

"This is highly irregular. I can't say that I'm happy about what happened."

"I had the honor of getting to spend the night at the equivalent of Mecca for the dragon race. It is a memory that we all agreed should be cherished and protected. You could court-martial me and still, I would protect it. As would the others."

"Of course, I'm sure that all of you coming out of this with shields and swords that hold this charge and energy the dragons use to fight has nothing to do with this sudden loyalty." General Miller didn't sound as if he was impressed.

I held my hands up, trying to ease some of the tension. "I haven't asked them to keep the island a secret. There's no need to. No humans will ever find it. Most of my kind can't even do so without some guidance from those who know where it is. If a group of humans tried without one of us, you would all die from the magic that holds it safe."

"As you wish. I will put it in my notes that you stopped at a hidden dragon waypoint to recharge, refresh, and ensure the safety of all, and that it seemed to be of no great significance. It's the only lie I will ever tell for any reason, however. Is that clear?"

"Perfectly, sir." Lieutenant Douglas knew when a meeting was over. He got up and hurried out of the room, leaving me with the general.

"Thank you," I said when the general and I were alone. "I couldn't have protected so many without their help. We came very close to stopping the demon from succeeding too."

"It seems that you and I are allies in this fight. I am not oblivious to the control and respect you have earned. Every other time you have landed here and come into this tent, at least three dragons have come in with you to protect you. Yet today you stand in front of me alone and without fear."

"That's true."

"My men are no longer entirely my men. You've won them to your cause. And I can't fault the sense and wisdom of you doing so."

"It wasn't intentional, nor is it meant to undermine you,

but I'd be a liar if I didn't admit that I'm grateful for it and I will use it to my advantage. But I also make you a promise. I'm not looking to make any enemies, piss anyone off, or hurt anyone or anything but this demon and his minions. We can be allies and protect what matters to us both without a problem."

The general looked at me for several seconds after I spoke, almost as if he was reassuring himself that I spoke the truth. Eventually, he broke eye contact and stood again.

"So far, I think we can manage that as well, Your Highness. Thank you for keeping my men safe."

"Always," I replied and left.

I found Neritas, Flick, and Alitas waiting right outside the tent, none of them far from me and soon all around me again.

Although I considered flying back to Detaris, after being in the air for so long and carrying the extra weight of two people, I was more than happy to walk. My companions went with me, none of them speaking. Some civilians who didn't dare approach watched us from a distance.

I didn't meet their gaze, so tired that I was ready to fall asleep on my feet, but I wasn't entirely done.

"We need more people who can use magic the way I do."

We passed through the bubble that protected Detaris and the city came into view.

"Working on it," Alitas replied. "I plan on sitting down with some honor guards and Jace and Capricia as soon as you're safely in your tower and resting."

I glanced over at him to see him grinning. I'd just been

told to get some rest and stop fighting so hard to get everything ready. "Yes, Dad!"

Alitas jerked, and a blush showed he'd realized his mistake in the way he'd addressed me, as well as his relief that I had chosen to make light of it. It made me chuckle.

Although I agreed with him that I needed rest, there were two things I wanted to do first. "I need a couple of minutes to myself first," I said, more to Neritas and Flick than Alitas. "Need to talk to some people. I'll be safe where I'm going and then I'll come straight to the tower."

Although they didn't look as if they wanted to listen, both Neritas and Flick eventually gave in and flew off to get rest too. I could tell from the way they flew that they were exhausted, and I'd done them a kindness as much as I wanted to be alone for a moment. Alitas stayed with me as we walked deeper, but his focus was already elsewhere as well.

Once I was forced to fly, I didn't go straight to the royal tower but headed for the top level of the library. I landed in a small room that was familiar, and did so far more gracefully than I had the first time I had flown in. I had been chased by several city bullies the first time, when many of the younger dragons were put out by having a red dragon among them for the first time in a long time.

A particularly stern librarian was in the room, the same one as the first time.

"I need to find Ben," I said, echoing that first occasion in yet another way.

This time, however, she pointed to the door that led up and stood back so I could hurry through. She didn't look entirely pleased about it, but I was queen now and I'd saved her life on at least one occasion. I'd earned some slack.

I stepped into the large room upstairs and spotted Ben sitting at the familiar table, surrounded by books and reading them under a dim light that helped preserve the many old tomes in the building.

"I'm sorry, Red, I haven't found anything new yet. I'm searching as fast as I can, and the majority of the time there are several other dragons in here helping me—"

"It's okay. I'm not here to demand you read faster. I went to the isle of the ancestors and spoke to my grandfather."

"Your grandfather?" Ben stopped what he was doing immediately, concern for me taking over all his thoughts.

"It's okay. He was proud of me. But he also told me not to forget about Anthony's journals. That Anthony had recorded some information that we might want and need."

Ben didn't have to move far. His bag was sitting on the floor by the table, and he reached in, pulled Anthony's journal out, and placed it on the small table along with all the notes.

"We ran out of codes to try," Ben said, much as I had.

I smiled as I told him everything else that my grandfather had said, emphasizing that we might want to try codes that we had tried before but on different pages. I reached for the list of codes we had already used. On the back of the paper, I'd written down everything I had come up with before.

After giving Ben a big hug and yawning in his ear, I hurried away again.

This time, I flew to the royal tower, but I didn't go to

my bedroom. I wanted to find my mother first. Thankfully, she had seen the others return and was waiting for me in the living room. Reijo was with her, and they both hugged me, but then he made his excuses so I could be alone with her.

I told her everything, not holding back a single detail as I talked about how inadequate I had felt not being able to defend one of my own cities or stop the demon. She simply listened, holding one hand and squeezing it a little when I talked of anything dangerous.

As I told her about the meeting with my grandfather, I cried again, unable to keep the tears from flowing. She hugged me and cried with me for a few minutes.

"He definitely is proud of you, along with your father. I'm sure of it. As am I. But you need rest. It's clear that you're exhausted, and there is nothing you can do to speed any of this up but sleep now, my child."

I nodded, not intending to argue. In a world where I was called *Your Highness* now more than anything, hearing someone call me their child was the exact balm I needed to let go for a few hours and know that it wasn't going to fall apart while I did so.

CHAPTER SIXTEEN

Feeling much better for getting some rest and munching on some snacks left out on the dining table, I contemplated the best course of action from here. Ben had assured me that he would come to me if there was any new information that could lead me to an item. Neritas was lounging nearby and charging some items I had activated previously, and Flick was practicing.

Somewhere, Alitas was teaching Capricia, Jace, and others to do what we'd thought only red dragons could.

"How did Capricia take it?" I asked Neritas.

"She wasn't surprised there were secrets. Acted as if it made her right about everything all along. But after some talking it over, she agreed to keep the skill to herself for now. Understood that now is a really bad time to cause a panic among our people. She'll want them all told fairly soon, though."

It wasn't surprising news, but I hoped that we would have time to tell them ourselves. Capricia was an unpredictable dragon who would happily leak the information if she thought I wasn't going to do so when she thought I should.

I'd known that when Flick suggested her name, however, and I put it out of mind for now. It was more important that we trained our army for battle than that I worried what the dragon population might think of us keeping a secret we'd discovered by accident along the way.

With that pushed aside, it gave me some free time to train and work myself. I activated more metal and worked on a few pieces of armor for Neritas, wanting him to have the first few parts of a full suit like I did. Flick would follow, and then whoever was leading units into battle after that. I didn't do all the armor but turned my attention to more weapons and shields instead.

While I worked, Griffin arrived. He gave me a brief overview of everything in the city and how the elders were handling odd disputes in the dragon world here and there. Some cities in other countries were being met with more suspicion and less friendliness than others, and they were having to walk interesting political lines. No one had dared to attack us yet, though, and for that I was grateful.

After Griffin had updated me on the day-to-day stuff, he brought my attention to the subject of recruits for a dragon army or militia to defend each city. Since the city by Phoenix had been attacked, more of them had volunteered, including some from the devastated city.

It still wasn't that many, though. More of the messages from them were asking for protection and making excuses. Griffin told me with an apologetic tone that they were still coming from a place of fear and not support for the cities around them.

I could have throttled them all. This wasn't what I had hoped for my people. We were powerful and needed to work together if we were going to have any chance to defeat this demon.

"What progress has been made, if any, on finding out how to make the gate or kill the demon once and for all?" I asked, changing the subject so I didn't lose my cool at the dragons and declare some kind of forced conscription. I didn't have the manpower to enforce that either.

"Not much. The area by the gate is being studied. Now that it is vacated, the ground is being healed by some of the green dragons who were serving in the honor guard protecting it, and the US government is keen to explore the large hole left behind. It seems to be an unnatural phenomenon."

"But the ground is toxic. Are they working with us on it?" I asked.

"The ground is extremely toxic, and few green dragons are available. Most are here, fighting alongside you." Griffin frowned very briefly. It was a clear point of contention. If we were going to figure out how to imprison the demon again, we needed to give it priority, but we couldn't ignore the demon and let it walk all over everyone and everything while we tried to figure it out.

Before we got much further, Jace, Capricia, and Alitas appeared. I only needed to look at them to know that there was another attack somewhere.

"Where?" I asked as I got to my feet. My bag and everything I needed was less than two feet away this time.

"Nearby. The area is both human and dragon, and we had a few dragons there who were already eager to fight. I've got some heading there from the farmhouse as well." Jace had everything she needed strapped to her back, and I took in the determined look on her face. This time it was dragons she cared about in danger.

None of us wasted any more time. I ran out of the tower, morphed, and mentally projected to everyone I wanted with me the news. By the time I had flown out of Detaris and could be seen by the soldiers on the other side, the previous unit commanded by the lieutenant was all standing ready and in formation, facing Detaris.

I flew down and landed in front of them.

"Requesting a lift to the danger zone," Douglas said. A slight smirk played at the corners of his mouth. I tried not to smile back as I nodded.

"I assume you cleared it with the boss?" I asked.

"Didn't need to. Got a direct order to accompany and assist, if you'll get us there. If not, we'll get ourselves there as fast as we can."

"We've got you." I clapped him on the shoulder as more of my dragons flew down and landed. A lot of them stayed in dragon form and accepted the soldiers they had carried before.

It was crazy to see so many dragons, but even more from my own city came down, and some more soldiers stepped forward as well. I quickly allocated the extra men and women before morphing back into my dragon form as well.

With so many of us, I considered splitting us up to get a unit there faster, but I didn't know if it would make much difference when the faster fliers were already carrying extra weight and needed to be more careful by default.

I took the lead at first, pushing the pace as much as I dared, but Alitas and Jace soon caught up with me. For the first time in a while, we flew north, heading up the coast and toward San Francisco.

The dragon city wasn't as far north as that, but it was near a coastal town, and from what little I had been told, the dragons and humans were already working together.

With this being just about the shortest distance yet and allies already on the way there, I had some hope that they could hold out until we could rescue them. If nothing else, delay the enemy and keep the city or whatever building the demon was going for from crumbling as fast.

I couldn't worry too much about what I would find. I'd managed to save a lot of lives the last time I had fought the demon, and that was a start, although I hadn't been able to stop him from getting the item.

I felt an ache grow in my wing joints an hour into the flight and knew that I had pushed myself far harder in the last few days than at any other time in the past. None of us flew this much normally. Not even the city guards. And if I was feeling it, so was everyone else.

Despite that, Jace didn't let up but stayed in front of the group enough that she was setting the pace more than I was.

Although I considered telling her to slow down, I knew it wasn't much further now. Anyone who couldn't keep up would still join the fight soon enough.

I'd barely thought this when I spotted the city up ahead. The dragon city was to the south of the human settlement and had been swallowed up by the city over the years. It appeared at first glance as if the demon was heading for some inhospitable spit of land in between the two settlements, but the humans nearby had freaked out and there were shadow catchers in the streets.

The humans in the area could simply flee, as could the dragons. But neither did, and I soon spotted a small group of dragons down on the ground to one side of the land. They were guarding something and using a mesh of the shields I'd given them to hold the ground.

As the demon sensed he was close or making good progress, he swooped in to get a closer look, bringing more shadow catchers and controlled wildlife with him. They appeared to swarm the small group of defenders, making Jace growl and push herself hard again.

Don't get separated from us. We'll help you get to them in time. No sooner had I spoken to her than I reached forward with my mind and charged the ground around the group of dragons below and up into the air, trying to form a protective barrier.

It wasn't easy, and I didn't think I could hold it around them for long when so many forces were up against them, but it let Jace know she wasn't alone and that, just as I'd done with everyone else, I was going to do everything I could to keep them all alive.

Using a little more magic from the connection I had with the ancestors, I fed it to all of us to help us fly faster.

There were more strange creatures alongside the shadow catchers, handlers, and the demon dragon before me. More birds than we had seen the last time, despite how many we had killed, and what looked like a demonic version of coyotes. It gave him a larger army than ever and showed that while I had been recruiting and trying to get more powerful, so had he.

It was also worrying for the wildlife of the planet. If he was corrupting large swathes of it and forcing us to kill them, then it could devastate ecosystems for many years after we had defeated him. If we could.

I understood why he had been so hard to defeat before. It was like fighting an uphill battle against anything living that could be corrupted.

Despite my fears and the dread I felt at facing him again and not knowing if we would win, I didn't hesitate to attack. Once again, Alitas took on the job of distracting the demon, and Capricia took on the birds in place of Jace. Jace had one goal—to get down to the dragons she knew on the ground.

I flew down there, dodging the large demon in the sky as Alitas flew at him. He roared his anger and irritation again but didn't back down. The ground forces were struggling, but Jace soon reached them, diving down as a dragon and using the charge on her scales to knock back some shadow catchers and coyotes while the soldiers on her back shot at more.

When they'd reached the circle of dragons, the soldiers jumped off and into the middle. Jace transformed and touched down on the edge of the group before she threw herself into the fight.

You both okay with repeating that move? I asked the soldiers on my back, noticing that it had bought the fighters some time to regroup and get their line back together.

I got an affirmative from them and then swung down low, charging every inch of me and lashing out with limbs, wings, and claws at anything that came too close.

The soldiers shot a few times before diving off me and into the safe zone between all the dragons. I quickly took human form, turning as I did and landing at the front of the group. With my armor, shield, and sword ready to go, I threw myself into the battle, slashing and hacking at demons and corrupted coyotes.

Many of them hit my armor and shields, especially the animals. They were mindless and aggressive, but they only hurt themselves. Their teeth were unable to dent my armor, and my blade was sharp enough that I cut through them when they got close.

The shadow catchers' strikes were harder to handle. An errant tail caught me on the back of one leg and unbalanced me. I knew I would be sporting several bruises once this was over, but I continued to fight, knowing I was doing far more damage to them and the demon's army than they were doing to me.

My presence also caused a distraction and a focal point that kept the enemy back from the others while more and more dragons came in and landed. I soon had Neritas and Flick by my sides, helping to keep the worst of the attacks off as we hacked and slashed.

A vapor haze started to form as so many creatures became the vile gas so fast that it filled the air and no breeze could blow it away fast enough. I coughed, wondering what something like this did to the lungs and hoping that it wasn't going to corrupt any of us either.

No matter how many of the enemy we killed, however,

more kept coming. I felt out with my mind as I fought, trying to get an idea of what we were facing, and almost swayed under the overwhelming sensation of demonic presence. Besides what we could see, there were handlers, and the strange portals were spewing out more shadow catchers somewhere near the city.

While we had been fighting here and doing our best to defend what seemed to be their target, they had been busy creating a foothold to attack from somewhere else.

This fight was going to be the hardest one ever.

CHAPTER SEVENTEEN

With Alitas keeping the demon occupied, I had a chance to assess his plans, so I slipped back behind Flick and Neritas to feel out further. While they covered me, I tried to work out what his goal was. Did he intend to overwhelm us?

"I think there might be a cave somewhere with more of those portals in," I told Flick and Neritas a few seconds later. "We're going to need to shut them down."

"Are they anywhere close?" Neritas asked. I shook my head.

I could also feel almost ten handlers out here. The numbers were simply overwhelming. While the dragons had been the group we had aimed to bolster when we arrived, I noticed that they weren't the only pocket of resistance.

Other groups of people were also trying to fight back. They were shooting at anything that got too close to them. I could barely reach them with my mind, but I connected to their weapons anyway and charged what I could feel from a distance.

At the same time, I charged the ground around them, helping them keep from being injured while they aided us.

"Lieutenant, any idea if any more of your folks are going to help?" I wondered why the army wasn't already here when humans were being threatened.

"I believe they are on their way. Can you charge their weapons as well?" He shifted through the crowds of fighters, jamming his shield down in time to block a coyote that slipped through to attack him.

I stabbed it, killing it in an instant. Part of the body collapsed, leaving behind a corpse, but all the parts that had been corrupted became vapor in the same way the shadow catchers did.

Neritas booted what was left of the body out and away from us. I charged it, wondering what would happen. It somehow took, and the body glowed slightly and then hit another, which it knocked over. The second coyote yowled in pain and went down, and Flick finished it off.

"If more get here, I'll make sure they're good to kill these things," I said when I got a moment. "In the meantime, I need to deal with some portals. They're literally spewing out more of these hellish things every minute."

The lieutenant's eyes went wide as Jace stepped up.

"We've got this area now. Looks like Capricia is almost done too. We can hold it until she can get to us." Jace slashed at another coyote and stopped it from hurting another of the soldiers.

I was worried that if I left now, they would be targeted, but the longer I left it, the more enemies we would have to face. If I didn't reduce the numbers in this fight, we were going to run out of capacity before we ran out of demons to stop.

Two handlers moving this way made my mind up. I moved toward the portals via the handlers. If I could take those two out along the way, I could ease the pressure on my friends as I went.

I charged the area around the circle one last time and helped them defeat a bunch more of the creatures and injure many more.

It worked well enough as I fought forward with Neritas and Flick on either side. The demons couldn't put up any kind of fight to prevent us. The pain they felt at coming into any kind of contact with the charged ground was enough to force them to yield to us or be destroyed.

The handlers understood this well enough to come at us. With my disks, I targeted the handler that was slightly further behind. Neritas and Flick followed suit, matching my target and helping to slow it and spread the two out a little.

Tentacles flicked out toward us, and one of them knocked aside a couple of mindless coyotes before I turned it away with my shield and slashed the tip off. The handler screeched but the next limb was already coming at us from above.

I sidestepped, shoving a shadow catcher out of the way to make space. It almost unbalanced me, but another shadow catcher attacked, swinging its large tail, and it helped me go back the other way, even as it jolted me.

As we got further away from the others, more of the demons crowded in around us and slowed us down. Flick put his back to us to stop him and Neritas from getting hit from behind.

With more limbs coming at us and the second handler recovering, I had no choice but to use more of my power to charge the ground and push back the enemy around us.

It felt like a waste of magic to put so much into the ground, but it was the only way to keep us safe and move forward. I needed to get Neritas and Flick some armor sets as well, or get them to work activating their own metal.

Either way, it was no help now. We needed to get to the portals and shut them down before everyone was overrun.

I pushed magical energy outward and took a moment to verify everything around me was charged. The handlers kept coming, however, and I had the briefest respite before two more tentacles came my way. I dodged and weaved to find both of them severed and Neritas and Flick grinning at my sides.

With the demons held back from us and screeching in pain, my friends could aid me once more.

I kept it up as we charged the nearest handler. It had only a few limbs left to keep us at bay. Within a minute, it was dead and shadow catchers everywhere were hesitating.

The handler nearby paused as it tried to take over the job of his fallen pal and keep the mindless demons from being slaughtered or doing the wrong thing. It was a huge mistake. Neritas, Flick, and I sprinted toward it. Magical energy rushed along the ground ahead of us, pushed along by all three of us.

We hit the handler hard and knocked it back off its feet. We never gave it the chance to get back up again, but chopped at limbs and worked as an efficient trio.

Another set of shadow catchers joined the first. They seemed more dazed for having had another handler try to force control for a moment.

We kept our momentum and rushed toward the source of the shadow catchers. With the armor, shield, and magic coursing through the ground ahead of us, we made far better progress, and I was soon near the first portal. Three more handlers rushed in to defend it.

I gritted my teeth as a large tentacle came at us and I was forced to slow, still thirty yards from the first portal. The demons crowded in around us again.

For the first time, I wavered in my resolve. I was aware of the drain on the magic we had. I had been pulling on my connection with the ancestors for power, but for the first time, I was feeling that drain, as if I was drawing more from them than they could sustain over time.

Worried it would be a permanent over-drain, I slowed my demand from that source, but it simply increased the need to pull magic from the other dragons and myself. I was already siphoning some, but I wasn't near that many dragons anymore, and they needed theirs to fight where they were.

Despite the fear that I had overextended myself, I was forced to focus on the moment and fight the shadow catchers and handlers closest to me with what I had.

I defended Neritas from a swish of a limb that would have caught him off guard while his attention was on an attack from another handler, but it caught me hard and knocked me down onto one knee. Grunting in pain and attempting to slash at it, I stayed where I was for a moment.

Another tentacle came at me, taking me by surprise.

I flew sideways as pain flared in my side. It knocked the wind out of me, making it hard to process, and the sun seemed to blot out as shadow catchers rushed me from all sides and more and more tentacles flew my way. I rolled and stabbed, only half-seeing what I was attacking.

Blows rained down, bringing pain with them, but also damaging every beast that made contact. The magic in the armor was diminishing fast as it hurt every demonic attacker.

I tried to get back to my feet, but I was in too deep. Somewhere, I could hear Neritas and Flick yelling my name, but it was barely audible over the screeching chaos of the shadow catchers.

Eventually, I got a handle on the magic again and pushed it out from me, drawing on the ancestors again to blast the enemies into vapor.

Blocking another tentacle and severing it brought me enough respite to finally get back to my feet. Neritas and Flick fought their way through to me.

Before they could reach me, several dragons flew over and down, landing beside me and scattering the demons some more. They transformed into humans as more flew to join the group I had left behind.

Capricia was soon standing beside me, sword in hand and shield up.

"Come on, Red. I've got those birds dealt with for the most part. Do I need to help you with your part of the fight too?"

"Whatever means we win," I replied. I had no ego in this and was grateful she'd shown up when she had.

With her, three city guards, and Neritas and Flick, we could form a proper group again and get back into the fight with a decent team.

I got them into a circle and deliberately stepped out ahead of them to push us forward and toward the nearest handler. Yet again, we were chopping tentacles, shoving back shadow catchers, and sending them back where they came from.

With the extra help, we soon had the handlers taken care of and had the space to press toward the portals. Although I couldn't see them, buildings nearby were spewing forth shadow catchers and I felt the strange presence in the houses. I moved toward the one that felt the largest and also happened to be closest to us.

It took a while to get up to the door, and then we seemed to stick in the gap. The shadow catchers were coming through fast enough that I couldn't get in through the doorway. With it only being wide enough for me, I struggled to get enough momentum.

I noticed Capricia move toward the side of the building, stretching the group out in that direction, but I was already committed to trying to get through the door. It did create some clear space behind me, however, as the group cleared out the demons in the area for a moment and I could prevent more from getting out.

Before I could get through the door, Capricia dove through the window and caught herself on her shield and rolled. I realized what she was attempting and charged the floor into the building along toward her. I hadn't wanted to use the energy, but it pushed the demons back enough that another dragon could follow her and I could finally step through the doorway.

We continued to fight on, gaining ground again. Though the building looked like a small apartment from the outside, the interior was an open plan that had no furnishings in it.

I spotted the portal almost immediately and connected to it. It was so large that multiple shadow catchers were rushing out at a rate we could barely contain, even as we pushed forward and I charged the ground.

Pumping all the energy I had barely made any difference. The portal was so strong that it fought back. Neritas and Flick came to join me and connected with it as well as the shadow catchers vaporized under all our attacks.

It was enough to turn the tide and get the portal shrinking. As it did, the flow of enemies slowed until some of us could stop fighting and take a breather. The building was secure enough that no one was going to surprise us.

Despite the victory and the satisfaction of feeling the portal pop into nothing, it had taken an enormous amount of magical energy and further depleted the armor and weaponry I carried.

While the fighters with me dealt with the last few shadow catchers in the building, I drew a little on the ancestors' connection to begin recharging the parts of my armor that were most depleted.

"One down, two to go," I said as we regrouped outside. "Though these two are smaller."

"Good job they are. I'm not jumping through any more windows." Capricia grinned at me in spite of her statement.

We threw ourselves back into the fight, killing everything in our way. We fought over to the next portal. The area was far less congested now that we'd dealt with the big one.

We spotted a large window that had already been busted by the shadow catchers coming through and decaying the wood and brick.

"Look, Capricia. They did your job for you. They must have known you'd whine about it, and they didn't want to hear it," Flick said when he spotted it.

"They knew your big head was coming through and we'd need the wider space." She grinned back at him.

It helped lighten the mood as we all threw ourselves back into the fray. Despite the sass and insults, Flick and Capricia were the first two to fight through the window while Neritas and I headed through the door.

Either because the portal was smaller and spitting out shadow catchers slower or because we were entering from two places at once, the attack was easier.

I'd connected to the portal to start shrinking it when I heard a strange noise from outside again.

"What was that?" Capricia asked.

Flick moved back toward the window as I focused on the portal anyway and carried on fighting.

This one was easier to shift and start shrinking. I still pulled a little of the magic needed from my connection with the ancestors, but it was a more sustainable amount, and the rest I took from the items on me.

The diameter had shrunk to about half the size, no longer wide enough for a shadow catcher to come through, when a loud bang sounded from somewhere nearby. It was followed by the screeched roar of the demon.

This time I knew what the noise meant. The demon had found what he was looking for. Another artifact.

I growled my frustration as I tried to decide what to do. I needed to stop him, but I was close to getting another portal shut. Choosing one option would make the other impossible.

"I've got the portal," Flick said. "Leave someone to watch my back and catch the demons coming in, but I can keep it shrinking."

As I slipped my mind and magic away, the progress slowed, but he was right that he could supply enough on his own now that it was smaller and it was going to continue to shrink, even if it was slower.

I left two of the city guards with him, but Neritas refused to leave my side. As it was, I knew that if Alitas wasn't locked in battle in the sky, he would be appalled that I had so few honor guards and official protectors like Neritas with me. I was better equipped than anyone, however.

Once I was out of the building, I leaped and transformed.

I spotted the handler carrying a wrapped artifact within seconds. The original group of dragons was between it and the demon, and Alitas and his unit hadn't let the demon get away from them yet.

For a second, I was torn. Did I get in between the demon and his prize and form a barrier of my own, or did I help the dragons who were already in the middle?

I decided to do both and aimed for the air above the

dragons and soldiers who were fighting hard on the ground.

I raced forward, but to my irritation and the detriment of all my fighters, the handler proved to be a far greater adversary than I had planned for. He was some kind of magical shifter I'd not come across, and he grew wings and flew up into the air like a demonic Pegasus. Before we could reach him or I could get close enough to throw magic at him, the handler was above the crowds and flying out to sea.

The demon let out another loud roar, this one very much of triumph, and flew up and out of combat. He used his magic to propel himself forward as fast as he could after the fleeing handler.

I tried to use magic to speed myself up this time, as well as put up a barrier of charged air. The latter was too hard to do, given the distance.

I drew on all the magic available to me, but I couldn't catch the demon, yet again.

I roared my anger after the demon. I had come so close to stopping the demon this time. Unbeknownst to Jace's dragons, who had gotten here first, they had been guarding *almost* the right patch of similar buildings.

With their leader fleeing, the handlers started to pull the army back, and shadow catchers turned and fled. I did the only thing I could in this situation and landed again to begin healing the wounded with the magical energy we had left.

CHAPTER EIGHTEEN

By the time everyone was stable and I had healed the most injured, there were reporters, officials, and more of the army had shown up. They had all been too late to help or record the main part of the fight, but that didn't stop them from acting as if they knew everything.

The army tried to command dragons to move places, debrief, and all sorts of other things. The dragons all joined me and informed the army that I was in charge and that any commands had to come through me.

A man wearing a soldier's uniform approached me a short while later.

"Are you Scarlet?" he asked, the irritation clear in his voice.

I was still healing a soldier who had taken a couple of nasty hits, and I didn't want to give this newcomer my attention until my charge was stable and no longer in pain.

In the few seconds I delayed, Lieutenant Douglas stepped up. "She's addressed as 'Your Highness' and is the queen of the entire dragon race, not Scarlet."

"And you are...Lieutenant? Are you trying to skirt the chain of command?" The soldier raised his shoulders and chin slightly, clearly ready to turn this into a pissing contest.

"Lieutenant Douglas of the new First Mythical Defense Division. I report to General Miller, and I am following his orders to work with her highness, Queen of the Dragons, and act as if she is my direct superior in combat situations in which General Miller is not present." Douglas stayed relaxed as if he was explaining something as simple as the number of siblings he had and how everyone knew them.

The newcomer looked as if he could have hit the roof, but somehow he managed to keep any emotions he wished to express under wraps. He turned to me.

"Your Highness, Queen of the Dragons, my apologies for not addressing you correctly." He barely paused to see if I accepted his words, and launched straight into whatever he had come here for. "We need to get to the building that housed the item the demon took. Several dragons are in our way and are insisting that we can't walk on US soil because of some silly claim that it belongs to them."

"That's because it does belong to them. The demon was targeting one of my dragon cities. My subjects are able to admit and refuse access to anyone they wish in their cities."

"Can you overrule them?"

"Of course I can. I'm their queen and they answer to me. But I won't."

"My superior is insisting that I learn what they were after and why."

"Great. I can answer that question, although I've already

forwarded all this information on to General Miller. The demon is trying to collect several dragon-created artifacts that were used to defeat him long ago and lock him behind the gate in the first place. We scattered them across the world among our dragon cities at the time."

"The first attack was in Denver." The soldier stepped back a little. His confusion took some of the sting out of his earlier aggression.

"It was. There used to be a dragon city there, but for some reason, it was abandoned."

He didn't respond immediately, looking thoughtful, but it didn't last before he was shaking his head and growing agitated again.

"So where are the rest of these artifact parts? We need to defend any humans caught in the crossfire."

I sighed, having already explained a lot of this once and not really wanting to do it again. I had people to help. "We don't know. I have my best dragons working on figuring it out, but these objects are powerful and my race separated them for a reason. To keep the entire world safe, they made sure that no single dragon knew all the details. Turns out that a bunch of them died without passing on the information."

"Well, that's incredibly stupid." He sneered, looking as if he was going to give me a dressing down.

"The gate and that demon have been where they are for thousands and thousands of years." I felt defensive over my ancestors and the choices they had made. "How much knowledge and information does your race have from before a thousand years ago? Could you find an artifact that had been deliberately hidden and limited in location in only a few days?"

He didn't reply.

"As soon as we know the location of the artifacts, you can be sure the US Army will be the first to know," Douglas added, backing me up.

I tried to focus on healing again after he walked away, but the majority were now healed, and I was running low on my own magic. I'd tried to avoid pulling more from the isle of the ancestors as I was afraid that it wouldn't recover. It had diminished during the battle, but it felt as if the connection might have begun growing stronger in the hour or so since.

Despite it all, I put on my best impression of a victorious leader and encouraged and thanked everyone as I moved to the edge of the dragon city and the rest of the warriors who had gathered from each race. Douglas came with me, seeming to take his self-professed instruction to stick to me and follow my orders to heart enough that I suspected they were very true.

"First Mythical Defense Division, then?" I asked him.

"Yeah. Someone higher up figured we needed it now, and I volunteered after seeing you on that very first fighting video. The one at the restaurant with that enemy who starts off looking like a dude and then...very much not."

I nodded, not needing a reminder of the fight. It had been the first very public fight, and I had only gotten through it and kept everyone alive because I'd had my mother with me.

Near the other dragons healing was a sight I hadn't

expected. Several reporters were trying to get an interview with the dragons present, persistently asking questions of several of them despite being ignored. Jace was the one most targeted, possibly because she had been seen with me in a lot of battles, but she had her back to the reporters and was simply encouraging the dragons to repair, heal, and get back to their work.

If it irritated the reporters to be ignored, they didn't show it. When they saw me approaching, however, they turned their attention straight to me. I was mobbed by at least five of them, along with their cameramen and several photographers.

One shoved a microphone into my face. "Scarlet, can you tell us what was happening here?" Although none of them were a threat, I instantly felt vulnerable and reached for the magic connections I had to suck in energy to defend myself.

It took a moment for me to think straight and realize that they weren't going to do me any harm and were simply overeager humans.

Trying to ignore them for a few seconds, I looked toward Jace and gently worked my way through the crowd. The reporters gave way. None of them seemed to want to touch me. I couldn't blame them when I was wearing my battle armor. It made me look more bulky and intimidating.

"Fill me in on progress," I told Jace as I got closer.

"The city is going to be fine. We lost two dragons before any help got here, and I am pretty sure that several humans are dead as well."

I winced at hearing a kill count. It hurt to think that

people I was meant to protect were no longer alive. At the same time, it brought back the frustration that I didn't know where to go to defend my people until they were already under attack. I might not have liked the soldier who had come to me and demanded answers, but I could understand him.

"Are the injured all stable?" I asked.

"Yes, and the city is working on repairing its shield so it can hide again. But there isn't a dragon here who truly understands how it works." Jace shrugged, and I wasn't surprised.

All the other dragons I had brought into this fight slowly joined us, including those Jace had sent in ahead. Everyone was healed and had expended what was left of their magical energy trying to aid the city.

Alitas appeared to be the most eager to talk to me, so I went over to him to lean my head in and discuss what had happened.

"Are you okay?" he asked. "I saw you take some hits."

"Nothing that the armor didn't turn for me. Maybe a few bruises." I didn't mind the pain. I had a few aches, but no decay from the monsters, unlike almost every other single dragon or human who had fought with us.

"That demon is…impossible. I understand why our ancestors opted to lock him behind a gate instead of trying to kill him." Alitas shook his head as if disappointed in himself.

"As long as you are all unharmed. We will find a way to lock him back up again." I didn't voice my desire to destroy him instead. I had no idea if it was possible, or if it was irresponsible to want to try when no one else seemed to know what to do with him.

The reporters continued to follow us, occasionally shouting questions and trying to get people to engage them. For the most part, they were ignored, but Alitas eventually nodded over to them.

"There could be merit in talking to people. If you want more human help with these fights, then getting them to understand some of this might help," he said.

"What if it makes them scared or if they blame us for this mess?" I asked.

Alitas placed a hand on my shoulder. He looked me in the eyes and set his jaw. "You won't have them hate you or blame you. You're a very likable person and they've seen you fight for them again and again. Take the lieutenant with you. I'm sure his support of you will help."

It was a sound piece of advice, and I called the soldier over. He hadn't gone far, but was using his men to help repair and lift and carry until we saw fit to carry them back to their base as well as return to our home.

"Okay, we can answer a few questions," I said when the lieutenant was with me and we were standing in front of the reporters. They'd grown animated as I'd come over, as if they sensed that I might say something, but I seemed to catch them off guard with the direct offer to cooperate now.

A reporter to one side of me was the first to recover his voice. "What caused the attack today and the one a few days ago in Denver?" a male reporter to one side of me asked, the first to recover his voice.

"There have been three attacks," the lieutenant

answered for me. "All of them looking for the same things and attacking humans and dragons alike who were in the way."

I thanked him internally and elaborated on his answer. "The demon is looking for something that could be used to defeat him. Trying to get to it before us. We're doing everything we can to find the locations he'll target before him and put defenses in place. We almost succeeded today, and we're getting closer to working out what he's after before him."

"Many lost their lives in the attack on Denver. Have there been deaths here as well?"

"The attack on Denver took us all by surprise, but it's not happened again. We've been able to prevent a lot of deaths in both the attacks since. Sadly, some have died here as well as in the second attack—which was purely on a dragon settlement near Phoenix. We're continuing to work with the US Army and other dragons to put early response teams in place around the country and then the world as well." The words came tumbling out of my mouth, but I had no idea if they were good enough or not. How did I brush off death?

"I know that every person who has died was a loved one to somebody out there. I wish I could give more than my condolences to those in grief now. But I will work tirelessly with whoever I need to and whoever wishes to aid us in trying to ensure this doesn't happen again and no more lives are lost. I have every willing dragon helping where they can and trying to figure out the demon's targets so we can preempt the attacks."

"How is the US Army acting to ensure the safety of its citizens?" one of the women shot at Lieutenant Douglas.

"I can't speak for all their strategies, ma'am, as it's not my purview, but I've been assigned to the First Mythical Defense Division and given direct orders to aid her highness in defeating the demons whenever they strike and however they strike. We are combining our forces for the maximum protection possible and I'm sure the army has other plans and strategies that will be deployed as they can be."

"So the government is recognizing the dragons' claim to sovereignty, even on US soil?"

"Of course," I replied before anyone else could. Even if it wasn't true, I needed to make it clear that I considered myself to be in charge and powerful, as well as an equal to their leader. "I am the leader of an incredibly powerful race of dragons all around the world and offering to ally with the US government against an enemy that has already killed both our peoples and a significant amount of wildlife on top. It only makes sense for us to put all awkwardness, differences, and other worries aside to ensure the safety of everyone."

"How many dragon cities are there?"

"Hundreds," I replied. "But I think that's off-topic for today's questions. I know you'll have many questions about us, how we've been hiding so long, how numerous our race is, what our intentions are, and so on. And hopefully, in time, these will be answered with our actions if not our words. For now, all I feel I ought to say is that it has been our assumed job to protect humanity from evil for thousands of years. We will continue to do what we can to fulfill that brief and defeat this demon once again."

"You've defeated him before?" the first man asked. The reporter round-robin was seemingly complete for one cycle.

"Yes. A long time ago. When dragons walked the earth more obviously, and there were more of us. A lot of the information on how and what that entailed has been lost. But, as I said, I have dragons tirelessly working on figuring out everything so we can do so once more. Now, if you'll all excuse me, I need to get back to Detaris with the information we've gained here."

Before any of them could ask another question, I backed up and walked away. The lieutenant quickly followed, but I didn't dare look at him. I didn't know if I had handled that well or not.

I wanted to get back to Detaris and I needed to get answers myself. No more waiting around for anyone to help me.

CHAPTER NINETEEN

I had never been more relieved to see a place than I was when the area around Detaris and the army base being built beside it came into view. The feeling of being home here was growing stronger with each passing adventure away from it.

Flying back had also given me time to think more. I was still resolved to figure out the remaining locations of the scattered artifacts, but I also wanted to keep pressuring dragons and the US Army alike to aid more in battles and prepare for possible strikes.

Although I understood my people wanting to keep dragon city locations under wraps, and no one had asked us yet for the locations of all of them, it would soon become a necessary disclosure. Just as I wanted dragons ready everywhere, so did I want US soldiers ready in every location that might be hit.

The only consolation was that the connection I had to the ancestors had fully recovered and I felt confident drawing magic from it to recharge everything again. As such, by the time we arrived at Detaris and were circling to land, the armor, shields, and weapons the soldiers wielded were all fully charged and ready for combat once more.

I landed in front of the army base again. The main tent blew in the breeze from the shore until so many dragons landed and blocked the area that nothing could get to it. Once the soldiers had dismounted, we all turned back into human form and the breeze could blow once again. By then the general was hurrying out toward us.

"Welcome back. Are you all unharmed?" The concern in his voice was genuine, and it made me like him more.

"All present, accounted for, and healed already of any minor injuries sustained." Lieutenant Douglas stiffened his back as he made his official report of duty.

"I've seen some of the news reports already," the general replied after giving the lieutenant a nod of acknowledgment and focusing on me. "It looks as if they're praising you as the world's first real superhero for what you can do in battle and how you rescued everyone."

I shook my head. "I'm no superhero. Just another person with power. A different kind of power, maybe, but it comes with a price, a weight, and... Well, you know the sentiment."

Douglas chuckled and nodded. "Great power. You're using it wisely. Trust me."

The vote of confidence made me smile, but I was still eager to get back to Detaris, get some food, and give the command I'd decided on before I went to hunt down the information I needed myself.

Thankfully, the general didn't keep me long. He simply wanted confirmation that everyone was alive. We hadn't stopped the demon, but we had made progress and learned more about the enemy. The general was also grateful I had charged up all his men's armor and weaponry again.

Although I was fairly magically drained, I also charged up some more of the gear lying around, doing it almost automatically before informing the general I had done what I could.

This seemed to win him over more, and he soon ended the meeting.

"Go get some rest and take care of yourself, Your Highness. You should be proud of what you're achieving and how well you lead your people." The general bowed slightly, almost awkwardly, as if he wasn't sure it was something he should be doing but had opted at the last minute to do it anyway.

I took his hand and shook it as he straightened. "It's an honor working with you, General. I hope we can keep finding ways to work together and make our people safe."

I walked away, ushering my dragons back to Detaris again. Once more I stayed as a human. I was tired of morphing and wanted to take in the city while I issued my orders.

"Let's get as much metal activated and charged as we can," I told Alitas, Neritas, and Flick after we'd let everyone else go ahead. "And train up the others some more. If they're getting the hang of it, choose more dragons, but let me know who they are."

"What are you going to do?" Neritas asked.

"I'm heading to the library as soon as I've seen the elders and get them to pressure the other cities more. I want to find out where this next artifact segment is before the demon does and beat him there."

"You should rest as well, as everyone has been telling you."

I shook my head at the suggestion. I knew Neritas meant well, but I couldn't afford to. Not this time. Thankfully none of them pushed it any further and allowed me to go about my task. I finally morphed back into my dragon form long enough to go up to the elders' chambers and report back.

Although I didn't have to tell them anything that had happened, I took the time to let them know what it had been like. Griffin was with me, the other elder to aid me in battle. My mother had been in charge while I was gone, and she quickly hugged me and checked I was well enough, another reason I didn't mind stopping in with the elders.

Once again, I stressed the importance of the cities learning to defend themselves, and I informed them how much more equipment could be sent out. It was a huge undertaking to train and equip so many dragons, and the elders were in a difficult position, so I didn't take more of their time than necessary.

I entered the library, and the librarian pointed me to Ben and moved to open the door for me.

"Thank you," she said quietly as I passed her. "I have family in the city you protected today. You saved their lives."

I nodded, a lump forming in my throat. Although I'd known that dragons had moved from city to city in the past, I didn't know how common it was. It was the first time someone had thanked me for saving someone specific. A lot of what I did and the risks I took went entirely thankless.

"I hope I can keep everyone safe in the future," I replied as I gathered myself.

"You'll never be able to save everyone, especially without enough help. But you're making a difference. And that's what matters most."

She didn't give me a chance to respond further, but walked away and went back to putting books on shelves and checking whatever archiving system she had.

I climbed the stairs up to Ben and found him fast asleep with his head on the small worktable he had been using. Beside him was a half-full plate of sandwiches, and around him were so many scraps of paper, scrawls, notes, and attempts at translating the journal Anthony had left for us that it was obvious he had been working at it until he had succumbed to exhaustion.

Doing my best not to wake him, I tried to work out where he had got to and if he had managed to translate any more pages. By his checklists, he'd tried an interesting system, going through all the pages and trying the same word that began a phrase to see if it produced anything that made sense.

Doing this, he had gotten a couple more random pages in the journal and begun translating them. That also let him know that the same phrase could be used to translate the next few pages after each of these as well. It resulted in a patchy decoding that gave us several pages out of context.

I read through those first, getting more insight into how Anthony felt about me and what he was discovering. He truly had cared for me and wanted to provide the most support he could. It was clear that he knew I was the daughter of the king and had been hidden away to keep me safe.

Once again, he mentioned working for someone, but not whom. And he mentioned not knowing where my money was coming from and wanting to find out. It also talked a lot about Jace and working with her so-called terrorist group. If I had been able to translate this part sooner, it would have been useful to take to the elders. They had proved to him that where I was concerned, they could be trusted.

Several times, it hinted at him looking for as much information as possible and trying to learn as much as he could so he could one day teach me everything I needed to know.

By the time I had read all the pages, tears were tracking down my cheeks. I had never missed Anthony more, nor wanted to tell him how grateful I was for the care he had shown me. When I'd found out that he had known I was a dragon and had kept it from me, I had gone through a mix of emotions and had mistrusted him and my memories of him for a while.

Now, all I felt was love and gratitude for a dragon who had given up time with the love of his life in the attempt to keep me safe and learn everything he could to help me. He'd known it was dangerous and he had done it anyway.

I sat to continue the work using Ben's tactic, being quiet to let my friend sleep. We'd have gone faster with his help, with two journals between us so we could work at the same time, but I knew how hard he had been working, and let him rest.

Once he was awake and clear-headed again, we would make good progress. And until then, I had the fort.

Over the course of the next few hours, I found one more phrase that was starting to work, but I was far less practiced than Ben at actually decoding it. It took me several more hours to translate all the pages for each phrase. It wasn't until I was translating one near the end that I found a journal entry that gave me hope.

Anthony had been given an old book by someone and looked through it with them. He mentioned it almost falling apart and how he couldn't read everything, but that he had gotten a couple of photos of some important details. In an attempt to preserve the contents in more than one way, he had written it down.

When his journal mentioned it being a rhyme, my heart thudded in my chest and my hand began to shake. Was this what we had all been looking for? The ancestors had told me to try this. My own grandfather had come to me to get me to work this out. Had I needed to be the one to sit here to do this all along?

I didn't know the answers to those questions, but I knew I was finally going to get answers from this journal, and right when I needed them the most. Despite the fear and excitement building up inside me, I did my best to focus on the translation, putting together a rhyme that I hoped was talking about the artifacts.

> *A dragon king's decision made*
> *To ever use again, he forbade*
> *The weapon, crown, and defense combined*
> *Of precious ether, metal, and gems refined*

One goal they had on Earth to protect
One foe designed, his attacks to reflect
Too powerful when their task was done
Broken up and scattered, all undone
Placed in ten, their pieces protected
Information on all never to be collected
Ten great dragon lords tasked to take
Across the world over mountain and lake
Five nearby, half within reach
Another two upon a distant beach
One given to safety in the tallest peak
With its twin buried where the Earth
  does leak
The final part the key of all
Kept safe with the strongest one standing
  tall
Where each may be guarded, no purpose
  known
The existence hidden and secret by him on
  the throne.

With the last word written and Anthony's confirmation that this was the entire rhyme, I sat back. Translating it had taken a long time, and my head hurt from working for so long in the dim light, but I finally had something to work with.

On many levels, I felt disappointed. How was this going to help me find out where the ten pieces were? It was obviously talking about the artifacts used to defeat the demon, but none of it mentioned where they might be beyond vague descriptions of terrain and in how many different places they lay scattered.

Already the demon had found three of them, and I was pretty sure that they would have been three of the five that were nearby. It didn't narrow those down, however. This was maddeningly unhelpful.

I was reading the rhyme for the fifth time, trying to figure out if I was missing something, or some kind of code within a code, when Ben finally stirred.

"Scarlet, how long have you been here?" He reached out to me with both warmth and concern.

"Long enough to continue your progress through to its goal. Sort of."

When he looked confused, I showed him what we had.

Immediately he grabbed another piece of paper and copied it out again. I lifted an eyebrow, confused by his behavior.

"I want to make sure this never gets lost or destroyed again. Although I didn't mention this earlier, it's looking likely that someone here has betrayed the city and damaged or taken some of the books in here. I can't find where the exact discrepancy lies or who could have done it, but I want you to put a copy of this safe, as I will. And not with Anthony's notebook."

Never one to argue with Ben when something had got to him, I did as he asked and tucked a version in my pocket to hide later. I could already think of a couple of places I could put it that no one else would find it. For now, I had more pressing thoughts, however.

"It's not enough to get us the locations we need," I said. It wasn't clear enough.

"Alone, no, not at all. But it's not all the information we have." Ben gave my shoulder a squeeze before he got up and hurried down the nearest aisle of books.

I got up to follow him, but he soon pulled a book off the shelf and came back. Faded in the leather cover, I could make out the words *A Genealogy of Powerful Dragons*.

"Remember when I said that we should try and work out the time frame that the cities would have been in play so we could see which ones were most powerful?" Ben asked.

"Of course. It's about all we had to go on."

"Well, we can combine that information with the powerful dragons alive at the time in this book and the cities that would have had the capability to hide something so precious, and the descriptions of terrain in the rhyme, and see what we can marry up. I can then look into that city more specifically and double-check that it could have been somewhere to hide something so powerful without the residents being able to sense it."

Ben's explanation left me with more questions, from the knowledge of powerful dragons to residents being able to sense the item. So far, all I had ever been able to sense was the enemy. Was there some way to pick up on a powerful object?

No matter how much I wanted to ask, I pushed the thought aside as Ben flicked through the genealogy book and tried to find the relevant dragons. He went straight to a particular section of time, almost three thousand years earlier. The dragon calendar didn't reset when Jesus had been born, like in the majority of the world. Instead, it was one long count from the dynasty of the first dragon who had united us all against the common enemy.

"Here," Ben said after a couple of minutes. "A powerful dragon lord is listed as ruler of the city near Denver at the time of this rough defeat of the gate demon."

He pushed the book toward me and showed me the reference. I read it a few times, wondering what good it did me, but I didn't know what good anything was going to do yet.

"We can use this to help find the others and the other cities." He grinned at me like it was obvious and was an answer in and of itself. With nothing else to do and no other lead, I moved in closer to figure out who else might have been alive.

Much to my surprise and relief, there weren't a lot of powerful dragons listed in each generation in the book, and we soon had matched up the other two dragon lords with the dragon cities already targeted.

"Here," Ben exclaimed a few seconds later. "I think we've found it. A city with a dragon lord who was powerful and whose city had the space for something like this underneath it. It sits near Las Vegas, out in the desert of Nevada."

I gulped. Would it be easy to find, or would we be able to get there and work it out before the demon showed up? And what if he went to one of the other cities first?

"I know there's still a lot of unknowns. But… I think it's worth taking a team of dragons there first thing in the morning."

Not sure I wanted to wait, I shook my head, but Ben

took my hand and stopped me from leaving with the information.

"You need to be rested and fully powered. In case he does show up or it's protected by powerful magics." Ben didn't let go of me until I nodded and agreed to get some sleep first.

I knew he was right, and I would do it, but I didn't like it. To have a location and not be rushing toward it immediately made me stressed. What if he still got there first? I arranged for someone to be contacted in the city we were heading to. They needed to prepare.

Finally, I confirmed that the relevant people knew we would be flying out first thing in the morning. Including General Miller. I didn't know if he'd give me any men to help, but I had to hope.

CHAPTER TWENTY

Although I hadn't slept very well, trying had at least helped recharge my own magic and given me time to think through a plan for where we were going.

Like some other cities in the dragon world, this one was far smaller than it had once been, and much of it was unpopulated and had been left to go to ruin. While it was a shame to see the cities fall into disrepair, I knew that it would make my job easier today. I could take a team of fighting dragons and soldiers and get on with the job.

If the demon showed up while I was searching it, I would have the best dragons possible to fight him off and not many to protect who couldn't fight or make a difference. It would allow me to focus on kills and taking out the enemy forces.

Everyone grabbed breakfast to go, and I met all my forces down on the ground in front of the army camp. I had the biggest force yet: all the honor guards, half of the city guard, and all of Jace's forces, including Elias—

although Sarai had opted to stay in Detaris and help distribute the metal we were creating elsewhere.

I also had the others who had volunteered in the past, like Griffin and Jared, and dragons from all around the cities who had been informed and wanted the chance to help and take on the great demon again. Ben and Reijo had also opted to come along, more as advisers and dragons who knew what I might be looking for.

After feeling as if I had to beg to get any help, it made my heart soar to see so many willing to fight with me and so many of them now better equipped to handle the fight. More and more had swords, shields, and armor parts that would help them stay alive and use magic on the enemy.

It would take the pressure off me if they could charge weapons and normal shields during any battles themselves, although I still hoped that we wouldn't have to have one of those.

Despite the extra dragons, the general didn't give me any more soldiers, but I did spread them out so my dragons tired less and no one had to carry two. The lieutenant practically insisted on riding with me, and I didn't object. He'd had my back in and out of battle several times now and I would have chosen to bear him in flight even if he hadn't chosen it himself.

We'd talked about harnesses or a saddle, but nothing was ready yet and I didn't want to try something new in this situation, so all the men and women who were coming with us had to hold on tight and agree to let us know if they needed to rest.

With everyone settled and the largest team I'd ever had ready for action, I rose into the air and led the party onward. Although Alitas normally led and we kept out of the way and flew high enough that the general public wouldn't find us easy to spot, today I led us and we flew lower, letting people see us.

I was on a mission, and this time it wasn't in reaction to an attack. This time I was trying to prevent one. And I wanted the world to know that I was making progress.

Despite not knowing where the city was exactly and having never been there, I felt as if I knew where I was going, and Alitas never corrected me. Since the boost from the isle of the ancestors, I thought I could also feel a small connection to each city. It was very faint and might be better described as an awareness of all the dragons in the world.

As I grew close, the feeling became more obvious. I knew that I was flying toward dragons, and I realized I also could feel how powerful they all were. Without the previous forced connections I had been using, I could feel the magic in those around me. Some of the comfort I had been feeling from being able to draw more from the ancestors was really coming from the powerful magic in those around me.

The city had a shield, much the same as the other dragon cities, but either it was failing or something had led to them underpowering it. Even a mile or so away I could see the outline of what I was aiming for.

As I swooped down to come in low, the city off to the side of a road and not that far from Las Vegas, I noticed that it worked perfectly to hide the city from down low. It was clearly weak in some way and the human population had thankfully never noticed.

No sooner had I landed and transformed than a small green dragon flew down from one of the more tidy-looking towers that made up the city. There were no defenses here anymore. What had once been a stream or lake that ran around the entire city was now nothing but desert sand.

The green dragon transformed and stood before me. He was an older man now, slightly hunched over and as short as his dragon had seemed small.

"Welcome to our city. Havilah used to be a wonderful place of beauty and power, but I am afraid that many of the dragon families moved on from here and you find only a few of us left to maintain what we can."

"It still holds plenty of charm," I replied. "Although I am concerned for your defenses if there was an attack on the city."

The dragon nodded and motioned for me to follow him, walking along the hard-packed sand. He pointed out where water had once bubbled up in a spring and filled the city with a lake of fresh water.

"It changed hundreds of years ago now, and in my memories, it has always been as you see it."

I listened to the elder ramble a little longer as he showed me and everyone with me deeper into the city.

"I'll get some eyes in the sky in case trouble comes," Capricia whispered to me as she surveyed the destruction that time had wrought. "We're going to want as much warning as possible if this place is attacked."

I couldn't disagree with her. If this city was attacked, it would be difficult to defend it, even with the small army I'd acquired.

"I know that you are proud of your home, and I would love to see as much as possible of it while I'm here, elder, but I confess that the urgency of my mission here has me eager to find the artifact stashed by the ancestors in your vaults and take it from here to bring you and your families more safety. I would also like to see if there's something that can be done to get the water back around the city."

"My men and I might be able to help there," Douglas replied. "We can't help with anything magical, but if there's a blockage or a manual solution, we're used to some sweat and effort."

For a couple of seconds, the elder merely blinked in surprise, his frail form frozen as his gaze flicked between me and Douglas.

"You really want to help the city get back to its glory days?" A hint of excitement raised the pitch of his voice.

"Yes, elder. To keep the shadow catchers at bay if nothing else."

"Please, call me Bartholomew. I am forever in your debt for even trying to care for me while you're here." He bowed to me, and instantly I felt awkward and unsure of myself. I had no idea what to do with this kind of attention.

"Bartholomew, it's an honor to meet you. Please lead the way to the vaults where the artifact might have been hidden, and then if you could aid Lieutenant Douglas and any dragons who think they can help in getting a handle on what might have happened to the water, I'd appreciate it."

Once again he bowed, and I found myself hoping that he wouldn't do it again and it wouldn't be far until we were in the right place.

We didn't need to fly as he led me along the sand and

weaved through the towers. They were similar to those in Detaris, but wider and older looking. This was a truly ancient city.

"The vaults are meant to be in this tower," he said eventually, stopping in front of the widest one. "Or under it. I don't understand the magic entirely."

I nodded, already looking for a way in, but I couldn't find one on the ground level—or any other level I could easily reach. Anyone going in was going to have to fly up and hope the internal structure of the tower was still intact.

Worried that we only had so much time, I leaped and transformed. I had so many dragons around me that I almost didn't get the clearance, but one downbeat of my wings had me airborne and flying up the side of the tower. I spun as I did, finding a door off to the left about six floors up.

I circled the tower a couple of times and took in the lack of other openings until much, much higher. It looked like a bridge had once connected this tower to another one nearby, but now there was just the opening, and no light source to see what was beyond.

Landing on the ledge, I turned back into my human form and tried to stand there. A part of the floor broke away, almost pitching me forward into the darkness. I managed to grab the side of the doorway in time to stop myself from dropping.

When I felt more stable and sure I wouldn't need to dive backward and take dragon form again, I used my magical abilities to make a light and try to see what lay beyond.

There was no floor, and the staircase that had gone downward was mostly crumbled. A few bricks stuck out around the edge of the tower, but nothing else.

"We're going to need some ropes," I called back to my friends. The tower was too small for any of us to take dragon form inside it.

My call aroused Alitas, who flew up as well and landed beside me. He also almost fell forward, making more of the stone bricks crumble.

"This is very unsafe." He frowned as he looked at me, as if he wanted to tell me to get down.

"It's very old and not looked after." I had no intention of letting anyone do this over me. If it was dangerous because of the state it was in, then I was the best equipped to survive it. I was wearing full-body armor and I had managed to get out of being buried alive once before.

On top of that, if there were magical protections, I was also the strongest dragon present and the one who could counter them best. I might be the one that everyone else wanted to protect, but I was also the best dragon for the job.

I called for rope again and didn't let anyone else come up until we had one secured to something on the ground. I tied the other end around my waist and watched Alitas as he looped the middle over himself and around his own waist the way a climber might when they were verifying that they could take the weight of another.

"I've got you," he said. "I'll feed the rope as you go and make sure you can't fall."

Knowing that anything Alitas said was as good as done, I took the first tentative step downward, shifting my weight gradually onto the bricks that had once supported the stairs. At the same time, I borrowed a trick from one of my first adventures and turned my hands into claws. I dug them into the walls to help take some of my weight, although it wasn't as effective as it had been on trees.

With the combination of Alitas holding the rope, and my own claws, I felt fairly confident as I made my way down the steps. I was safe enough that no major harm would come to me.

I made myself glow and soon found that the stairs were more intact further down the tower, and I could walk down them normally.

"It's better down here," I called up before undoing the rope. "Help some of the others down. I'm going to keep going a little further."

"Be careful of traps," Alitas yelled back. His voice was slightly muffled. I could also see a central support pillar now, and the stairs sometimes joined with a platform that must have once been part of a floor.

I felt out with my mind for anything magical, as I tried to do everywhere, but so far there was nothing strong other than the feel of the dragons.

The doorway had been about six floors up, but I felt as if I went down far more twists of stairs and past more platforms than that. After a couple of minutes, Alitas caught up with me and insisted on being by my side. I slowed, wanting to be more careful if others joined me so that nothing would harm any of us.

It gave more of the group time to catch up with us, until Ben, Reijo, Jace, Neritas, and Flick were also with me.

Capricia was the last to join us. She'd rounded up a team with every color dragon in it as well as a couple of repeats.

Now that we had all the equipment we did, it didn't feel as important to have a dragon of every color, but it brought me some comfort. This team—with the exception of Reijo—was the one I was most familiar with. Reijo normally acted as battle support for my mother, but he was here for me now and that mattered a lot to me.

All I had to do next was find this artifact piece without getting any of us killed.

CHAPTER TWENTY-ONE

As I reached the bottom floor of the tower, I exhaled with relief. It had felt as if we were trekking downward forever. I guessed we were a long way under the city, but it didn't feel cold, as I'd expect from going so far underground.

I still couldn't feel anything magical besides the dragons around me and the now faint presence of the dragons we'd left above. They were the only thing that gave me a rough idea of where I might be. It was a good way below them.

A tunnel opened up from here. It was wider than I'd have expected, spreading out to something broader than the tower itself. As we walked down it, stones began to glow as if they were reacting to our presence. It allowed me to stop draining my magic to make myself glow.

I tried to figure out where the danger was going to come from. I guessed that these artifacts were all guarded somehow, not just buried away. They weren't meant to be retrieved again without a serious cost, according to the notes Anthony had made and the rhyme he'd recorded.

Although I hadn't seen where the second and third artifact had been taken from, I had seen the first one's resting place and I knew that it had been protected there too. I also knew that the demon sent in handlers, but not how many had perished in the attempt to get them, or what they had needed to learn or solve.

In our battles, I had killed so many of his minions that I was sure he didn't care about them. They were all cannon fodder, though some were smarter and more capable than others.

I cared about everyone with me, however. And I wanted to keep them all alive.

Alitas wanted to lead the way, but I wouldn't let him. I stepped everywhere first. We followed the hallway deeper under the city and away from the city of people nearby.

Up ahead I could see a room with a big sand-colored door across it. It had once been ornately carved, but time had worn away whatever picture had once been there. Time and neglect, like everything else in this city.

I walked slowly up to it, motioning for everyone else to stay back a little in case I triggered a trap with too many close by.

Nothing happened and I stopped in front of it, not sure how to open it yet. I took a deep breath, closed my eyes, and focused on the magical energy of the area. I felt the very faint sensation of something on the other side and another twenty meters or so beyond. It was weak and hard to connect to.

I focused on it, worried about connecting to something I couldn't see after the last misadventure I'd had with a magical source on the other side of a shut door. It had sucked energy out of me until it filled up a well enough to unlock the mechanism holding the door shut.

I almost hadn't had enough, even after drawing on the sword, shield, and dragons with me. But it had spat it all back at me as I'd closed and locked the door again. This felt different. It wasn't connected to anything, and it didn't try to pull on my magic or encourage me to connect to it the way that door had.

Confident that I was feeling the artifact through the door and nothing else, I pulled my mind back and moved my hands to shove at it. As I did, I noticed something not quite feeling right inside the door. I paused with my hands an inch off the sandstone. Something didn't feel right.

I felt for whatever it was with my mind. Something was in the door, but it didn't have any magic in it. It felt like the natural energy of anything had been removed. It was so subtle that I'd missed it for the more obvious magic source further in.

Alitas came a little closer. "What is it?"

"There's something inside the door…" I frowned as I considered how to explain it. "It's like it's a magic dead zone. A magic black hole."

"Like those disks were when that handler threw them back to us?" Neritas asked, also shifting closer.

I nodded, grateful for the reminder. That was exactly what this felt like.

"So it's going to suck energy into it if we touch the door?" Flick asked. "Just those two tiny disks sucked all the power out of your shield and some."

"This could take unknown amounts and might be difficult to disconnect from once connected." It didn't bode well. They'd made it hard to get through this door.

"Let me do it." Neritas stepped forward. "You can break the connection and haul me out of here if it goes wrong.

I shook my head and put an arm out to stop him.

"Let's at least see if we can go around it first," Alitas replied, a smirk on his face. "I prefer to bypass traps rather than deliberately trigger them."

This sounded like a better idea, and I concentrated on the object again, trying to work out how it impacted the room and if it was just in the door. I quickly felt the tiny ribbon of it going out around the walls and encasing them. It seemed to spider cross with other threads, some of which went under the floor and over the top. There was no gap big enough.

"Well and truly impenetrable," I said after telling them what I could feel.

"So the only solution is to overload it like we did your disks. They could only absorb so much before they reverted to normal." Flick shrugged as if this was the simple answer to the problem.

"But we don't have a clue how much energy it could take." Alitas didn't budge his stance. "It could drain all of us and everything we have."

"What choice do we have?" I asked a few seconds later. "We have to get this artifact and there's only one way in."

The silence following my words was thick and heavy in the atmosphere. No one could argue with me, and the longer we took debating it, the more we risked the demon showing up and taking our choice away.

"Keep an eye on me," I said to Alitas and the others. "I'll

try to draw on the magic in my connection to the isle of the ancestors first and then the kit. I'll only feed it magic from all of us if that runs out and I think we're close."

"What if it doesn't let you break the connection until it's satisfied?" Neritas' hand went to my shoulder.

"Then you get me out of here as fast as you can and fly me away. Connections don't hold forever." It wasn't a great plan. The connection I had with the isle of the ancestors held fast over enormous distances, although it grew weaker further away. Maybe if they got me back to Detaris, even if I couldn't break the connection, its pull would be weak enough that the combined magic of the dragons there would be enough to at least keep me alive.

Of course, I didn't voice that last part. I hoped this wasn't going to go wrong and I wouldn't have to be rushed out of there before it drew on more magic than I had.

I took a couple more seconds to psych myself up to touch the possibly lethal door trap before I connected my hand with the door. At first, it felt as if nothing happened.

Then it was as if it suctioned my hand to the door and connected right to the center of it.

Pain flared and I winced as I felt the magic start to drain from me. I immediately sucked it from the connection with the ancestors and gripped my sword in the other hand, in case it wasn't enough.

The door trap was so hungry that it swallowed all the energy from the connection I had to Kilnar and even more on top, pulling extra from the sword. The flow was so fast it started to feel as if my insides were burning and all I could do was hang on for the ride.

I gritted my teeth as the pain built. The magic flowed so

fast it was burning a channel through me and there didn't seem to be any sign of it slowing.

"Red, talk to us. How bad is it?" Capricia and Jace also came closer, and I was sure that if I gave any indication that I couldn't cope, both were about to yank me off the door.

"It's not puppy dogs and roses, that's for sure," I managed to say between sharp breaths. "But I can handle the magic amount for now."

While I kept an eye on the sword, feeling more coming from my weapon as the magic drained from the isle of the ancestors and diminished the flow, I also tried to check the trap.

Magic was clearly flowing into it and spreading out across the net in pulsed waves that traveled around to the back of the room. It gathered somewhere at the back, like there was a well there, but it sucked up so much so fast that it seemed to pool and spread out along the strands.

It gave me hope that if I could keep the flow up high enough I could overwhelm the system and break it. As the pain continued and time ticked by, I grew used to it. As long as the magic supply didn't fail on me, I was going to be able to keep it going.

My connection to the ancestors didn't hold out much longer, however. It slowed to a trickle in comparison to what was being sucked out of me. I reached for the shield on my back as well, starting to suck magic out of that but leaving my armor alone for now.

With the sword and shield bearing the brunt of the pull, I was worried they would quickly run dry, but I felt the magic spreading and the net in front of me getting overwhelmed.

I was making progress, and I couldn't give up. I closed my eyes as I felt the sword drying up as well. The net was about two-thirds covered, and the magic was still flowing into it and through it. Something on the other side felt as if it was pulling magic out as well.

It was hard to concentrate on anything but giving in to the demand, and I had no choice but to connect to all the armor I wore as well and let it take from my final line of defense in battle.

Neritas was clearly monitoring what I was doing. "You're going to drain everything dry." I glanced at the dragons with me, noticing that Alitas, Jace, Capricia, and Flick all looked equally concerned. They were the ones who also had the ability to connect and feel the flow.

The net was almost full when my shield and sword ran out of energy entirely and I was forced to consider pulling magic from dragons around me. Before I could ask any of them if they were okay with that, Neritas placed a hand on my shoulder.

Almost immediately, his hand stuck fast to me as the trap tugged on the connection with him as well, pulling it through me. He started to pull it from his sword and shield as well. It was almost a relief, and I could have sworn that the trap drank it and spread the magic around the net faster.

"Quick, Alitas, Flick, do the same," Neritas said through his gritted teeth. The names sounded funky but recognizable enough. They followed suit, and as the burden eased again my mind was able to clear. The pain, however, grew worse as more magic flowed through my hand.

When Jace and Capricia worked out what was happening and added their hands, stretching around the guys to reach me, I almost screamed at the increase in flow. Magic poured from all of us and every charged item we were connected to, flowing so fast into the net that I could see a glow of light shine from it.

Ben came closer as if he was also going to touch one of us. "This had better work soon."

"Stay back," I called toward him, knowing he wouldn't understand why he couldn't help. I didn't doubt that without the ability to channel the magic that we'd taught the others, he would have nothing to draw on but his own magic supply and would get himself killed before we were done.

Ben did as he was told and Reijo along with him. I exhaled with relief that they were safe, but the feeling was short-lived. I'd hoped that the magic suck would stop when it reached the central node that was connected to us directly, but it didn't. If anything, the pull intensified, lighting up that one point more.

I whimpered, in agony now and desperately wanting to pull my hand away.

"You're almost there," Ben called out as if he finally understood what was happening. I didn't feel as if I agreed with him, especially as the last of the magic flowed from my armor. It was no longer able to come from me or the magic supply I had within.

I felt Jace and Capricia running out as well. They both had less in their arsenal in the first place. Worried for the safety of my friends, if not me, I tried to pull my hand off the door and put a stop to the drain. The pain tore through me. My hand was stuck fast, kept in place by a vice-like grip.

"The only way my hand is coming off this is if we chop it off." I hoped nothing so drastic would be necessary.

Something seemed to finally give. The device in the door screeched and started to whir, using some of the energy to turn a mechanism somewhere. At the same time, it latched onto my hand harder, although not more painfully.

The net shattered. The sound of breaking metal, more audible than expected, echoed through the rooms and the earth around us.

Less than a second later, the magic that had poured out of me came slamming back, flowing into me and threatening to overwhelm me. I grabbed all the connections I could from all the dragons around and flowed the magic back into our equipment to fill it and them.

Significantly less magic came back than had been sucked out of us. The items were getting about three-quarters of what was taken, and none of the magic that I had pulled from my connection to the ancestors came back. I hadn't tried putting any of that back, but I didn't draw any more from that source for now either. The supply was so weak now I didn't dare.

A fraction of a second after the magic flowed, back the door swung open and admitted us into the place.

The snapping net of metal had broken some of the walls. Parts of it had crumbled and grown weaker over the years anyway. We had to walk carefully, as dangerous shards stuck out all over the place. All of it glowed.

Despite the light from the metal, it was a dark room with no other source of light. I made myself glow, hoping to make it easier to see where the artifact might be, but I didn't need to look hard. Sitting on a pedestal in the middle of the room was a piece of metal that looked as if it might form the grip of a shield.

I went straight to it, stepping carefully to avoid broken metal shards on the floor, and picked it up. It was made of leather, and I half-expected it to crumble. Instead, it felt brand new with no signs of aging.

Although I didn't know what it did, I slipped it onto my arm. We had beat the demon to one of the artifact pieces. Finally.

CHAPTER TWENTY-TWO

Taking a moment to calm myself and collect my thoughts, I stood in the middle of the underground room and felt out with my mind. This had been one of the strangest moments in my life and I wanted to journal it later for better understanding.

If this was how all the artifacts were protected, no wonder the demon had put some effort into getting them. I didn't know how he fed the magic, but I knew it was costing him handlers to get as far as he did. Were they killing themselves trying to override these dangerous systems?

I had no idea, but I couldn't linger. We had to get this artifact away from the city and the demon had to know I had it so he wouldn't come here looking for it.

I led the group back the way we'd come, leaving the door wide open this time. I didn't dare put it back in case it tried to fix itself back in place and pull more magic from me.

While I had received plenty of magic back, I still felt

wrung out, and I knew it would take a long time before my connection to the ancestors was restored to its previous level. I walked gingerly back to the base of the tower and started to climb.

I felt the artifact on my arm, but I tried to ignore it, not wanting to try anything else new yet. I could figure out what it was capable of later.

It took me several rotations of the tower to realize that I could hear a commotion outside and people yelling. We were almost level with the ground again, and once more I reached out to feel the presence of others. There were shadow catchers in the area, and more flowing in fast.

"We've got company," I called, starting to sprint up the stairs. At the same time, I made my hands claws again and used them to grab the side of the tower and help move my body upward faster.

Under the shock of so much sudden weight, the steps started to crumble underfoot, but I was moving so fast they didn't slow me. I knew I was causing problems for the dragons behind, but I was more concerned for the soldiers and dragons I had left outside. The strongest fighters and most powerful magic users had come with me down the tower.

If the demon had arrived, my companions could already be in trouble, not to mention the dragons that lived here might need protection. I had thought it almost entirely abandoned, but there were at least a few who lived here and still called it home. More out of sheer will and determination than because it made sense to.

I had to climb the walls for the last few floors when the steps would no longer hold my weight.

The rope was still there, and I used it with one hand to give me something firmer to hold onto while I transformed my other hand and feet into claws so I could dig them in and get enough grip to climb.

Despite being more proficient at holding a halfway form, it wasn't easy to climb, and it made my limbs and claws hurt to use them like this. It wasn't normal dragon behavior to climb anything. I wasn't going to give up, however. I could hear the sounds of battle and shadow catchers screeching in pain and intimidation.

At the doorway, I threw myself out of it and took dragon form. I roared, looking for the demon, unable to feel his presence but sure he wouldn't be absent from this.

He was a long way off, way up in the sky, but he homed in on me as soon as he saw me. I didn't wait for anyone to join me but flew up to meet him.

Once again, he had corrupted an array of wildlife. This time, he had even more birds of a larger and hardier variety. They came straight for me and forced me to charge my scales and roll with my wings tucked in as I passed through the flock. I killed many of them on my way through, hitting them hard as well as tearing and clawing at them.

My momentum kept me going until I burst out the other side and could unfurl my wings again. I looked for the demon, but he had shifted and was behind me. I dove away from his attack.

You can fly, I will grant you that, his voice echoed in my head.

While you cower behind mere birds. I knew I shouldn't engage him, but I couldn't help it. I was more angry at him than I had ever been at anything. This demon had killed so many in his pursuit of power.

Am I that different from you? You cower behind water and walls. You've been hiding your whole life. You should be thankful. I have brought you all out into the light.

I roared my anger as I flew at him this time, but he used magic to make himself faster. I missed him, flying past and having to roll and dip to avoid a counterattack.

Red, where are you? Neritas sounded panicked.

Up, I replied, dodging as the demon came at me again. I had no capacity to say any more as I traded blows with the demon, both of us scoring a hit and draining magic from each other.

When he caught me again, a claw hit a scale and tore it off, and I could truly feel how much combat drained magic. Just as the door had pulled magic from me, so did contact with him.

Pain flared from the area now missing a scale as he dropped it to the ground below. I backed up, flapping to pull my body up and back from him. Before I could get away from him, the flock of corrupted birds came at me again.

I had no choice but to fall and tuck my wings in once more. Shifting into a dive, I gained momentum and let my speed fight the creatures. Some of them got lucky, catching the exposed part of me and hurting the tender flesh bared by the missing scale.

Once again, I couldn't see the demon, but I didn't panic. I tried to feel out for him with my mind. I couldn't detect him. I had no sense of magic where I thought he would be. All I felt were the shadow catchers and handlers on the ground, the birds around me, and more corrupted land animals coming up from the south.

I roared as I came out from underneath the flock and spread my wings to slow my descent. Neritas, Alitas, Flick, and most of the honor guard were there. Alitas was leading the dragons as they flew up and into the flock. Neritas and Flick broke off and synchronized as they came out the side of the flock and flew back around to me.

They need you on the ground, Alitas told me. *Get back down there.*

For the first time, I wanted to argue with Alitas. The demon wasn't like us anymore, if he had ever truly been one of us. He was something else now. More powerful. It made me wonder if he had been able to activate the artifacts he had acquired. I didn't know if he had a whole one yet, or parts of all three, but something was different about him.

I fed the information to Alitas, warning him to be careful. I did as directed and returned to the ground. The soldiers were still around the old spring area with some equipment I hadn't expected to see there and what appeared to be several civilians as well as the dragons trying to protect them.

The elder and the few dragons who lived in the city were forming another pocket of resistance, and the city guard from Detaris was trying to protect them inside a larger circle. They were moving further and further away from the vault tower, guided by Capricia's second-in-command.

I was torn on whom to defend. Both needed me, and I couldn't be in two places at once. My duty was to both. My dragons were a family of sorts, but the humans relied on us for protection.

I'll go help the city guards get the dragons out of here, Capricia said into my head, sensing my indecision. *Go help those soldiers get that spring working again and keep them safe while they do. It'll wipe out a ton of these vile creatures in one hit.*

Although I still felt conflicted, it helped me make up my mind for now. As I flew over to the soldiers, I noticed that a section of the shadow catchers was heading in an entirely different direction. A couple of handlers were heading with an entourage toward the tower and the vault I had pulled the artifact from.

It was a benefit in some ways to have the army divided, even if only a fraction of the forces, but it wouldn't last. When they found the artifact gone, they would come looking for it elsewhere. I had to get it out of there and get everyone else away from the fight as well.

I mentally kicked myself for not closing the door on the vault room after all. Maybe it would have slowed the enemy down and cost them more to discover the artifact fragment was gone.

I landed in front of the soldiers where the press of shadow catchers was worst. I used my bulk and the magic channeling across my body to crush several of the demons and then I spun, slashing and tearing with my teeth and claws.

I'd opened up a small area, so I transformed into my human form. Neritas and Flick did the same, joining me on the ground and taking as many of the demons down with them as possible.

Once we were all in human form and the last few dragons who weren't already part of a unit joined us—like Ben and Reijo—I got everyone into a loose circle around the soldiers and civilians. There weren't enough of us to form a tight circle, but we couldn't let the demons through to attack the soldiers. I charged the ground between us.

The soldiers almost all had shields, but several of them were still busy trying to solve the spring problem, and it was better for our fight if they could be free to shoot and not have to hold a shield wall against monsters far stronger than they were.

I excluded myself from the circle, intending to move where needed and cause as much havoc as possible. I was still the most protected of all of us, the only one armored from head to toe.

Neritas and Flick both had some pieces of armor each. Their torsos were covered now and they had metal boots on their feet to kick and stomp at parts of shadow catchers and the tentacle-like limbs a lot of the handlers had.

Sensing my presence, or maybe sent here by the great demon, several handlers came straight for me. I didn't have time to do anything but shift my focus to them and brace myself for the attack. I dodged the first tentacle and rolled under it to stab up into the second. A quick yank of my arm, and my momentum carried me into another roll that severed the limb.

It hit the ground not far from me, where it kicked up sand and made me cough. For a couple of seconds, I couldn't focus to fight. My body was at war with itself and indignant about having to breathe dirt instead of air.

Although I attempted to dodge, another swipe from a

tentacle caught me and knocked me off my feet. Hitting the ground made the problem worse, and another cloud of sand flicked over me. I rolled again and struggled to get back upright.

As I did find my feet, narrowly missing another hit, I noticed how hot I was getting. We were fighting out in the full sun, and I was wearing a heavy metal suit.

I could do nothing but sweat and hope that I didn't get too much sand inside the metal and start chafing on it. I already had a sore stomach area where the scale had ripped off. I didn't let it stop me from fighting, however. I needed to take out these handlers and figure out what to do from there.

I continued to dodge, duck, and weave, chopping more limbs off than I took blows while trying to fend off three of the creatures. Three more times I ended up on the ground, each one triggering a covering of sand and yet more grit and discomfort as it slowly worked into my suit.

With my focus on the fight and staying alive, I could ignore the dull pain it caused, but it took its toll on my ability to move. As I grew less graceful, another limb slammed into me. I managed to keep my feet, thanks to my sword lodging in the meaty tentacle for a few seconds.

I yanked it back and down and cut the appendage almost off. The handler screeched. It had only a couple of tentacles left on its body, and the most damaged of them was trying to end me.

I took the opportunity while it was vulnerable and ran at it, finding the ground still firm enough that I didn't slow too much. As I got underneath the reach of the remaining tentacles, I leaped and used my full weight and momentum to drive my sword up and into its head.

With a final cry, it went over backward, taking me with it. Some of it vaporized, but my sword remained lodged in the carcass. I tried to get up and yank it out, but it didn't budge. The two handlers remaining on either side of me were still swiping at me and didn't give me the opportunity to try again.

Forced to leave my sword for a moment, I rolled off the creature and back onto my feet.

I had no other weapon, I was forced to punch and roll, dodging more and using my shield to attack with or give a good thump. Without the magic, it would have been like trying to break a rock with a fist, but with the magic, it hurt them every time I hit them.

It wasn't ideal, however, and it took a lot more physical energy.

I needed to create an opening and get my weapon back. The handlers never stopped coming, however, and I was forced to react again and again.

CHAPTER TWENTY-THREE

As I took another hit that knocked me off my feet, I felt how tired I was. This battle was exhausting me in a way they didn't normally.

I got to my feet, spitting out sand, and then pulled back behind the circle of dragons while I got my breath. Looking around, it looked like everyone was struggling more than normal. Was it this heat? I couldn't think of anything else that was different.

As I looked around, I spotted a handler who appeared to be focused on us and not moving. Using my mind, I tried to work out what it was doing. My jaw dropped as I felt the connection that hadn't been there before. It was subtle and small, but the handler was drawing magic out of all of us. And it was exhausting.

With no other help and not knowing how to break the connection, I pulled magic from my armor and shield and fed a little to everyone around me, including myself.

I tried the only thing I could think of and reached for

the connection as well. I tried to break it off, but it was similar to the doorway of the vault. It was suctioned to me.

I felt a lot of pain as I tried to tear it out. I stared back at the handler from the center of the group and fought with him. Pain seemed to flicker across his face as well, and his eyes shifted as I refused to give up and tried harder and harder to break the flow of magic.

Finally, I managed it and he wobbled. It hurt a lot, and I didn't want to repeat it, but the handler didn't give up, already reaching for a connection again.

I kept buffeting it away. It was easier now that I was aware of it. At the same time, I reached for its connections with the dragons around me. One by one I mentally fought them, freeing all of them and stopping the handler from reconnecting.

With each liberated dragon, the fighting group around me grew stronger again, recovering and fighting harder, until eventually the handler appeared to give up and focus back on controlling his minions.

By the time I had everyone powered back up and Neritas looking out for similar attacks, the handlers who had gone down into the tower, decaying the structure further, had come back up. They knew the artifact was no longer there.

You've been very sneaky, a familiar chilling voice said.

I frowned, not intending to answer him. I'd been keeping the new artifact hidden behind my shield and not thought about it since I was so busy fighting off attacks.

I think you should hand that over.

Thinking fast and sure the demon was going to come

straight for me, I pulled it off underneath the shield, trying to hide what I was doing.

"Flick," I called. He was closest to me, and the best flier we had. He turned and came to me. It opened up a gap in the circle, but I took his sword from him. At the same time, I used our shields to hide handing him the artifact.

"Get this out of here and back to Detaris," I whispered so only he would hear. "I'll cover you."

A grin spread across his face as he strapped it to his arm, still hidden by our shields.

"You've got it, Red." Without another word, he launched himself into the air, turning into a dragon and flapping away and over the demons nearby.

"Hold the fort down here," I told Neritas as I followed suit.

It didn't take long for the birds and the demon in the sky to notice our presence, although I still couldn't detect him mentally. I could see him, and he clearly focused his attention on me, turning in the sky briefly.

What are you up to now, Princess?

Queen, actually, I thought back. *And your demise. No matter how many times you might think you have beaten me, I will keep coming until you're back behind that gate.*

I got only laughter back for my threat, but I meant every word.

You want that artifact. Come get it.

I wondered if the taunt was the right idea, but the demon seemed to buy it. He sent the birds toward me and followed close behind.

Flick was nearby, but already trying to speed away, flying underneath and to one side as the birds came toward us so he could get away. He made it a short distance further before a handler from the tower leaped into the air and started flying.

I roared a warning as it charged at Flick from the side and changed direction. Instead of heading for the demon to keep him distracted, I flew hard at the handler, charging the air between it and Flick. Whatever happened, I couldn't let him get hurt.

Flick managed to swerve in time, but a second handler launched into the air, and then the birds were on me, forcing me to fold my wings or have them torn to shreds.

By the time I was out the other side, Flick was trapped in between the two, and the demon was between me and Flick.

Letting out another roar, I charged at the demon.

Protect Flick. He has the artifact, I told Alitas when I realized I wasn't going to get to him in time. *He's trying to break away with it.*

We can do one better than that. Alitas flew between me and the demon as more of his unit dove down to help Flick.

The tables turned yet again. The dragons fought hard, but the demon understood our plan now and turned his attention to Flick. He hadn't gotten far enough away before the handlers had blocked his path. The birds came at him next as Alitas flew at the demon himself. I rushed toward Flick, attacking the birds and trying to clear a route for him.

With my scales charged, I snapped and clawed at anything I could reach and continued to thin the flock. I burst out the other side again and looked for Flick. He was flying and dodging, keeping himself out of harm's way, but never managing to get away.

The demon flew harder and faster to get to Flick, ignoring the rest of us, even when Alitas and Kryos flew straight for him and narrowly missed clipping him or snapping at his wings. I felt the demon sucking in magic and using it to power himself in the same corrupted way as his handlers and the vault door.

It wasn't a connection to anyone in particular, but it was bad news for anyone who had contact with him in any way. But contact was needed while flying in the sky. It was a way to have a huge advantage and the demon knew it.

The birds kept coming at me, making it hard for me to stay in the air, but I fought on, trying to get to Flick to help him and kill the birds in the meantime. After a while, the flock began to thin. So many of them fell from the sky that they littered the desert floor below me, and I was running out of energy of my own to charge my scales.

I had no choice but to pull on the magic of other dragons and take what little I could get from my connection to the isle of ancestors or go back to the ground and morph back to human form. Hoping that I was close to victory and making the birds less effective, I took energy from the dragons on the ground and the residents of the city, the dragons still trying to get away and out of the heat of battle.

I felt slightly guilty for stealing their power, and I drew as slowly as I could, still using some of my own. It kept me going as the contacts grew less and less anyway. Once I felt as if I could focus on Flick again, I flew toward him. Alitas and the honor guards were doing a good job of protecting him, taking hits and trading blows with handlers and the demon alike to protect Flick, but none of them could get him out and away.

We're running out of magic we can draw from in this form, Alitas told me. He was beginning to slow as several of the dragons with him dropped to the ground and transformed.

It left Flick more vulnerable.

Get everyone with a ranged weapon to focus on these blasted birds. I'll protect Flick.

I didn't point out how dire my own magic situation was as well. I had to get to Flick and protect him. The handlers were forcing him lower and lower as magic from the demon made them faster than Flick could fly. I roared to get their attention as I dove down and went straight for the strongest-looking handler.

It tried to dodge, but I raked my claws down its side. It bellowed in pain, and when it tried to turn to hurt me back, I tucked my wings in and rolled, giving it nothing but claws and teeth.

Thanks, Flick said. *I'm running out of magic too. Gonna need to land again soon. Recharge and try again.*

Get down with the others, I replied as the demon came at me and Flick dove toward the patch of ground Alitas was covering. Kryos and several other honor guards were already forming a protective circle, shields up and blades out. The more of them that joined, the more they spread out and started fighting toward Neritas and Jace.

As I dodged a dive from the demon I felt the magic pull from me and into him, something on him making it suck at my magic without needing to form a proper connection.

It made me lightheaded as I ran out. Only my connection to the ancestors saved me. The magic quickly replenished my complete lack, if only a little.

With everyone else on the ground or heading that way, I was the last dragon left between two handlers, the demon, the remainder of the flock, and my friends. I guarded them as best I could, roaring, snapping, and clawing at anything that came into reach.

I took hits as well. Scales came off and revealed the flesh underneath, but I wasn't about to give up. As a handler came in for what they thought was an easy attack on my midsection, I used a small boost of magic to twist faster. I sank my claws deep into their underside as they flew by my previous position.

I shook them mercilessly and pumped what was left of my magic into my claws to do the maximum damage. I let go when my vision started to go black and I couldn't stay in the air any longer.

With a final flick, I chucked the dead handler away from my dragons and out into the crowd of shadow catchers, squashing them and giving myself a reprieve to land. I hit the ground hard, unable to focus properly and taking a moment to change out of dragon form.

As soon as I was human, I collapsed and leaned over to clear my vision. Flick quickly crouched beside me and took my arm.

"You okay?" he asked. "You're bleeding in a lot of places."

I nodded, once again very aware of how wounds as a dragon translated to wounds in human form. We couldn't morph between the two without certain attributes transferring. Injury was one of them.

All of me hurt and blood was oozing out between sections of my armor, sand was everywhere, and I could barely stand.

"Stay where you are for a few minutes." Alitas' voice was more commanding than I'd ever heard before. "You just took one hell of a beating."

I didn't argue, but I kept slowly drawing on the one lifeline I had, pulling in what magic I could get from the ancestors. It was the only thing keeping me in this fight. My sword was gone, still stuck in a handler somewhere else, and I handed Flick back his so he could at least fight for now.

My shield was so low on magic that I was getting afraid to use it, and my armor was patchy where some of it had taken more of a beating than the rest. While I sat on the sandy ground, I tried to even out the magic, flowing it around and using a little of what I was gaining to at least add to my shield again.

I lost track of how many shadow catchers were killed while I sat there. The team around me had some of the most efficient fighters. The demon in the sky and his remaining flying consorts weren't out of the equation, however. Flick and I were still their targets, and it wouldn't be long before the flybys and attacks from the air became too much.

This fight was far from over.

CHAPTER TWENTY-FOUR

Getting to my feet again, I finally felt strong enough that I couldn't sit out of this fight any longer. I had healed myself a little while I sat and recharged.

"I need my weapon back and then I need to get that final handler out of the air," I said to no one in particular. At the same time, I looked for the corpse of the handler where my weapon was buried. There had been magic left in it, and I needed it. If I was going to turn this fight, I needed as much magic as I could get.

I considered taking the artifact back from Flick, but he was in better shape than me right now and able to move more easily. It was safer with him. On top of that, for now, the demon seemed to have forgotten about him in favor of trying to get to me. Every few seconds, something flew at me.

Most of the time, the honor guard deflected it before it could get to me, using the shields they bore like extensions of their arms, but now and then I needed to defend myself.

Each time, I turned the attack on my shield, but it made me struggle more. We had to do something differently. The handler didn't appear to be taking any damage from hitting charged metal, and we already knew that the main demon could heal himself in some way.

If I was going to help us, I needed to get my sword and I needed to get the two main groups of fighters working together and in one large circle that could defend the soldiers better.

As Kryos almost passed out and was sucked back into the middle of the group, I reached up and took his spear. It still had some magical energy in it. The honor guard second was still unable to manipulate magic and use it where it was needed.

"Need to borrow this for a bit while you rest." I looked him in the eyes. "I promise I'll give it back."

"Take it as long as you need. I've got your back if nothing else." He lifted his shield, but I could see how much that cost him and I reached out and lowered it.

"You're no good to me if you're too tired to move."

He opened his mouth to protest but eventually relaxed and gave in. He knew I was right. If we were going to endure this fight, we somehow had to rotate resting members and let those who were freshest fight on. While we had the artifact among us, the demon was going to keep throwing his entire army at us.

I stabbed toward the handler as it came at me the next time, and it veered slightly off course to dodge me. I didn't score a hit, but it gave Alitas the chance and he stabbed at it. His blade scored a cut to its underbelly.

The creature bellowed and pulled up short on the usual

flyby. I took the opportunity to push out of the circle and encouraged Alitas to follow me and bring the others. The shadow catchers almost all dove on me but I thrust with the spear, swept with the shaft, and shoved with my shield to close the distance between Neritas and me.

Unable to move to come to me or lose the ground the soldiers were still working on, Neritas could only glance my way now and then over the heads of the foes between us. His group had tightened their circle as fast as they could, having gained a couple of the dragons who had been in the air at the beginning. It meant he didn't have to keep charging too much ground between them all to keep the circle free of demons, but I could see him growing weaker.

Feeling guilt over abandoning him when he was desperate to never leave my side, I fought hard. Somehow, pulling magic from the ancestors and the spear Kryos had lent me was enough to give me the strength I needed to get across to Neritas and take out shadow catchers along the way.

There were still several handlers, but we'd killed enough of them that the remaining ones were being held back for now. They sent waves and waves of the mindless drones into battle.

Now that there were fewer different and confusing auras nearby, I felt the presence of several portals as well, and the animals that had been brought up to our rear somewhere were still there, being held in reserve. It terrified me how many minions the demon had. No sooner did we kill one of them than another popped into place and joined the battle.

No matter how much magic we had, we couldn't win

unless something changed on our side of the equation. There was too much to fight and we'd begun the battle with some of our magic drained. I had no intention of giving up, however. The soldiers were still working with the machinery they'd acquired while I'd been in the tower getting the life sucked out of me. While they hadn't given up and we still had magic left, I would defend the artifact we'd gained.

I kept moving, dragging my circle of warriors behind me. The gap slowly closed, until Neritas could shift with the fighter beside him and the soldiers could concentrate their fire to kill what was left between us. As we surged forward, our fighters moved through the gaps and filled in.

Alitas and Flick both took a break for a moment, stepping into the center of the circle along with Neritas, me, and Kryos.

"Any idea how Capricia is doing with the dragons who lived here?" Kryos asked, beginning to look a little better. He had a half-eaten candy bar in his free hand.

I shook my head. I'd been concentrating so hard on this part of the battle that I had mentally lost track of her. I reached out with my mind. I had drawn magic from some of the people she had been protecting, and more guilt hit me. I couldn't treat people as if they were batteries, there for my use, even if I was trying to save their lives along with everyone else's.

I could feel her, off toward the city and farther away than ever. They were near the edge of the mass of shadow catchers but I could also feel a handler near them.

"They're almost out and the vulnerable are almost at

the point where they can flee, but they are meeting some last resistance."

"Permission to take three others and go assist?" Kryos pulled a smaller curved sword from his pack. I held the spear out, but I felt the magic pulsing in the blade he carried. It might have been shorter, but it was far readier to do battle than the spear was.

He shrugged. "Give it to someone who needs it when you get your blade back."

Without waiting to see if he really did have permission or not, Kryos grabbed three of the honor guard who normally took a watch with him and broke out of the circle in the direction Capricia had gone.

I felt mixed about them being in the wild when they were such a small group, but the demon continued to focus on me and Flick as if he knew that Kryos was a small fry in the grand scheme of the battle.

With the soldiers better protected and a full group of fighters now working together, I grabbed almost the perfect squad, getting Alitas, Ben, Neritas, Flick, and Jared to accompany me toward the handlers that were left, and my weapon. Jace took command of the main group, giving me a nod.

As tired as the rest of us, she wasn't wasting words, and neither was I.

I hurled myself into the fray again, not used to using a spear but charging it with magic enough that it was deadly on contact. The demon and the handler in the sky continued to track our movements, hounding us.

Several times we were forced to duck and form a shield roof. The impact of the claws raking across it had many of us wincing in pain, but it kept us safe as we gained ground. It wasn't long before we were surrounded again, but the shadow catchers were quick to fall to a group like ours, even when we were exhausted.

The next time the handler came, flying low again to get me, I ducked along with everyone else, but at the last minute, I rose upward, thrusting against the claws with my shield as I rammed the spear up into it.

I was lifted off my feet and wrenched backward when the weapon stuck for a second. I managed to keep my grip on it, and a twist of pain from the handler dislodged it. I fell to the ground, landing on a shadow catcher that caught me long enough to take a hit from my charged armor and then vaporize.

Somehow, I was on my feet again, crouching to brace myself, the shield hitting the ground and stabilizing me enough I could parry the next shadow catcher's tail.

"How in the name of all dragons everywhere did you get that to look so damn cool?" Flick yelled as the group fought over to me and absorbed me again. The handler bellowed, trying to fly away but struggling finally.

"Shoot it!" I yelled, hoping the soldiers had some ammo left and could help bring it down.

The monster tried to circle and get back toward the demon, no doubt in the hopes of being healed. The few soldiers with the skill formed a line behind Jace and her defensive barrier and shot at it en masse, ripping a few holes in its wings and helping to injure it a little more.

As it sagged lower, I ran toward it, breaking from my group and using the shield to shove and batter the lesser demons out of my way. When I was still a few meters off, I threw the spear like a javelin, hoping to drive it deep into the creature.

I didn't stop as it hit and knocked the handler to the ground. The creature wasn't dead, but it floundered, unable to get into the air again, and tried to pull in its wings and twist to attack me. Some more shots from behind helped unbalance it and gave me the chance to fight past its defenses and grab the weapon again.

I pulled the spear free with a sickening squelch. The creature bellowed again and tried to turn to attack me. I dodged back and took a beak attack on the shield before I drove the spear down into its skull.

It shuddered for a second, almost pulling me off my feet before it went still, finally dead. The entire wing structure and face of the creature vaporized, leaving a rotten-smelling carcass that made me step back and gag.

I managed to keep hold of the spear, but I didn't use it in combat as the shadow catchers near me rushed forward, almost frenzied by another handler dying. Again, I used the shield to push them out of the way. My sword and the corpse it was still sticking out of were close by and an easy target.

Running as fast as I could, I covered the ground between me and the unmoving body and used the spear to practically climb the corpse, that was still only partially vaporized. After switching the spear to my shield hand and carrying it along my arm, I reached down and grabbed the hilt of my familiar sword.

Almost as if it was bonded to me, I felt the familiar magical connection and was grateful to find it still had magic left in it. It took magic-enhanced strength to get enough of a grip and twist on it to pull it free, but eventually it came out.

The blade was covered in ichor and the smell almost made me gag again, but I had my sword back, and that mattered more.

"Red, look out," Jace called a fraction of a second before several people called various versions of my name. I spun to see the demon coming in toward me. I was too far from anyone and standing on a handler corpse, more up in the air and vulnerable than I usually was.

I had one option this time. Brace for impact and do as much damage or more than I was about to take.

As I brought my shield arm up, I also stuck the spear out. It caught him in the side of an arm, but the damage was almost negligible as his claws punched through my shield and into my arm. I twisted as I was forced back.

Falling backward off the large corpse saved me from being hit even harder. Still, the pain as my arm was torn up stopped me from being able to move and I ate sand again.

While I was trying to recover, healing myself as swiftly as possible with the magic I had left, the demon banked around. I heard several people screaming my name and the sounds of battle, but if anything was close to me, it was quiet.

As the pain began to fade, I did my best to get to my feet. The shadow catchers near me didn't give me much longer to recover before they were attacking and trying to knock me down again.

I didn't dare parry with my shield anymore. The magic was almost gone from it again and it had three large rents in it, but I didn't let go of it. My hand gripped it automatically.

More and more shadow catchers came pouring in, getting between me and my friends as they tried to run toward me. I panted, aware of how exhausted I was and how much death was in the way of me getting safe.

I was in trouble. Big trouble.

CHAPTER TWENTY-FIVE

Despite the daunting task ahead of me, I ran toward the nearest shadow catcher in my path and stabbed it. The creature screeched and flailed, but I took several hits on my armor to do the maximum damage I could until it vaporized and I almost choked on the fumes.

By the time it cleared, I saw the demon again. He had come around to get between me and safety as well. The shadow catchers scattered, but some of them didn't get out of the way fast enough and were crushed when he landed.

It was the first time I had seen him on the ground, but he didn't take a different form. He stayed as a dragon as he stepped toward me. I tightened my grip on my weapon and considered matching his dragon form.

I knew how little magic I had left anywhere but in my sword, however. I was going to have to fight him as a human.

Not so boastful now, are we?

Doesn't mean that you're going to win, I replied, knowing I had nothing to lose at this point.

He laughed again and I wondered what it must be like to be so sure of yourself that everyone felt beneath you. Especially after you'd been locked away for thousands of years.

I didn't get very long to think about it as he rushed me, using his wings to get up speed across the sand. Even on the ground, a dragon could move fast. Our limbs were powerful and more than strong enough to bear our weight.

It took all my concentration to dodge at the right moment and strike at his flank before having to throw myself flat to avoid his wing.

I looked back to see if I'd done any damage. I knew I'd hit him at least—my arm still felt the jolt. He'd sucked some magic from the sword as it had hit him. A scale lay on the ground as he spun, managing to slow and turn faster than should have been possible.

The wound I'd created healed before my eyes, and a new scale grew right back.

He charged again.

At the same time, several shadow catchers came at me, so fast and aggressively that I knew the demon was controlling them himself. I dodged past one and shoved the second toward the first, and managed to tangle them. I used magic to speed my reactions and threw myself down, rolling under the demon to attack his underbelly with both sword and spear.

Again, I managed to hit him, but this time I wasn't so fortunate to come away unscathed. His tail caught me, and one of the spikes on it stabbed into my calf as he flicked my body out and to the side. I crashed into more shadow catchers. My armor sizzled as the magic was drained from it fast.

I rolled and slashed, trying desperately to get away from them and get a breathing moment to heal the damage done to me. One of the shadow catchers died, puffing out from underneath me and dropping me to the ground again.

This time I landed better, rolling in time to land in a crouch. It stopped me from eating sand for the millionth time, but I was still vulnerable.

When I tried to push up and onto my feet, the injured leg gave out and tipped me back down into a half-kneeling position. I leaned on the spear, gripping it and bringing the shield over the injured leg as more shadow catchers came at me. The demon paused where he was, no doubt to heal himself as well.

The only satisfaction I had as I pumped more magic into my body to encourage it to heal and continue despite the damage was that I saw more of his blood on the sand than mine. A lot more.

I was still faster and able to keep shadow catchers at bay when I was down and hurting. It drained yet more of my magic, however, and the little I was pulling from the ancestors wouldn't keep the shield going against many more attacks.

Somewhere in the distance behind me and over toward the human city, I heard shouts and the rumble of vehicles, but I couldn't turn to see what was going on. I was so pressed to fight that I had to concentrate just to stay alive.

I hoped that, if nothing else, it was the citizens of this almost ruined city finally getting to safety and that Kryos and all the dragons protecting them would be able to return to the fight.

No one had yet managed to get through to me, but I knew my friends were trying. Slowly, my leg healed enough for me to get back on my feet, although the pain was so bad I was forced to grit my teeth.

The demon roared again, and his shadow catchers pulled back slightly, warning me that he was coming in for an attack again. This time I didn't try to hit him but simply threw myself to the ground to get out of the way of any attack meant for me.

His tail hit several shadow catchers instead of me, sending them flying. It was a brief reprieve as I struggled to my feet again and looked for the source of noise and commotion. Despite my bragging to the demon, on the ground like this, with so little magic left, I couldn't defeat him. And he knew it.

Before he could make another run at me, however, five dragons flew in. Kryos and Capricia were among them. They landed beside me and transformed.

I immediately held out the spear to Kryos and leaned in closer to them. Their shields guarded me as we all faced the demon.

How sweet. More of you have come to die along with your queen.

None of us replied to the taunt, as far as I was aware.

"We don't have to hold long. More help is on the way," Kryos whispered. His eyes never left the threat.

The relief his words brought was almost too much to bear, and my body threatened to give way. I'd fought demons until I was tired before and my hands were shaking from holding my sword and shield. And I'd been hurt before. But this fight had been something else entirely. All the usual coordination and teamwork had gone out of the window as we were stretched too thin and pulled in too many directions.

If the demon heard the good news, he gave no indication as he studied our small group and then rushed to attack. With no discussed plan, everyone held their ground, shields braced in a line and weapons pointed out.

The demon's eyes widened as we continued to hold in the face of his attack, but I knew this could hurt. Stuck in indecision and not knowing for the best, I hoped the demon would balk and give way, but he kept coming.

As he came at us with his jaws open, mostly aiming for me, I was forced to throw myself backward so I wouldn't have my body impaled. Kryos came with me. I felt the movement and responded as he thrust the spear into the side of the demon. Capricia fell a second later.

The rest dove to the sides and attacked the demon's flanks, making him roar.

I rolled and scrambled to my feet again, trying to ignore the pain all over my body. It didn't take me long to notice that Capricia wasn't moving. She was still flat on her back, and her mouth was moving as if she was trying to say something but nothing came out.

I dove down beside her, fear washing through me.

The sand around her started turning red as I placed my hand on her chest and pulled all the magic I could out of her weaponry and mine to heal her. Her body responded and she reached up and grabbed my arm, her gaze shifting to my face.

"Hold on." I felt the sting of tears. "I'm healing you. Just hang on."

The demon laughed in my head as I tried to work. I ignored him, encouraging her body to repair itself. The pool of blood reached me, but I didn't move or give up.

Eventually, Capricia gave my arm a slight squeeze and gritted her teeth.

"You've got this, Red. Send him back to hell."

I shook my head. Her words sounded like a goodbye, but I didn't want to accept it.

"Red, on your feet," Kryos called, reaching for me. I shrugged him off and continued to heal Capricia and pump magic into her. Slowly her grip on my arm loosened and her arm flopped back to the sand. And the magic I was pumping into her did nothing. Her body no longer responded.

The magic wasn't helping, but I didn't stop trying to heal her, trying to connect to the injuries directly and give those parts of her body the healing magic. Kryos tried to lift me again, but I still resisted, not wanting to stop.

She's dead. Now it's your turn.

The demon's voice in my head did what nothing else could and pulled my focus away. As I stood and tried to focus on him, I realized how many tears were flowing down my face.

Capricia had spent this entire fight protecting those who needed it. She'd given her life trying to keep me safe. She didn't deserve this, no matter how much we'd disagreed in the past. Every decision she'd made had been based on doing her duty and protecting dragons as the captain of the city guard.

I stared at the demon as I pulled the magic back and out of all of Capricia's weapons and shield, making them useless though it risked her and them being decayed. Throwing my own broken and battered shield to the side, I lifted my weapon and, for the first time, stalked toward the large monster.

If it's the last thing I do, I'm going to make you regret ever taking on a single dragon.

It wasn't the best threat as far as threats went, but I saw the hint of uncertainty in his eyes before he lowered his head and charged at me again.

I didn't stop striding until he was almost upon me. At the last second, I hurled the sword at him and leaped upward. I transformed in the air.

With my claws, I tore huge welts in his face before I flew up and over him. With another flick of my tail, I smacked into one of his wings, tearing it and snagging it enough to turn him slightly.

The roar he gave off as he slowed and stopped in his tracks to fight back was more satisfying than any damage I had ever done to any monster.

I didn't stay in dragon form long. I wanted to be close and pull in more magic. I dropped to my feet and came around to face him again.

My sword was gone, however. I could see it sticking up out of his head. With no sword, I could only run at him and away from the shadow catchers.

Blinded and reaching up with his claws to pull my blade out of his face, he didn't see me coming. The sword wasn't in deep enough and dislodged, and he leaped upward and powered himself up into the air and away.

I went to follow, but Kryos grabbed my arm.

"You don't have the magic left and he can fly faster than you." Kryos didn't let go this time, making it clear this was something he was willing to fight over. "I won't lose another today."

Although I wanted to disobey him, I gritted my teeth and nodded. I didn't want to admit it, but he was right. I'd already come close to dying once and Capricia had paid the price for it. I couldn't be so irresponsible again.

The demon wasn't about to let us get away with hurting him so much, however.

"Duck," Kryos yelled as he brought his shield over both our heads and yanked me down to the ground. The sound of several thuds hitting his shield sounded as he grunted in pain. I raised my arm to help brace it for the last few, but they were less forceful anyway.

"Those damn birds." He got back to his feet, moving carefully so we weren't bombarded again right away. They were flying in a very tight flock, several more of them now dead around us, necks broken and faces smashed by the contact with the shield.

I shuddered to think of how innocent looking at a bird had once been.

Unable to dwell on it for long, I was pulled out of my thoughts by the rush of the shadow catchers again. They came in hard, seemingly boosted again. The demon wheeled overhead, the tear in his wing getting smaller as he healed himself as well.

Although I had access to more magic, my body had run out of the ability to heal any more damage and I had to be a lot more careful now. And I had no idea where my shield was. I still had my armor, but a few parts of that were cut up as well.

Despite the metal I wore being strong enough to withstand every type of attack, the demon had cut through it like it was butter.

Kryos didn't give up on me. He found my sword and handed it back to me as he kept his shield handy to defend both of us. The two honor guards who had flown in with him also gathered around me, forming a defensive triangle I could shelter in for a few seconds.

We tried to fight our way back to the few who had left the main group in a desperate bid to help me, but they were as hard-pressed and being forced back toward the main group of dragons and soldiers. Ben and Flick were as out of magic as the rest of us, and they were taking turns sheltering in the middle of their fighters.

I had pushed us too hard and had too few dragons and too little magic. Even after everything we had done, we were going to be overwhelmed.

The odds were overwhelming. The never-ending mass of shadow catchers and handlers, birds and portals made it impossible to win. And to make matters worse, the demon finally unleashed whatever corrupted animal he had been holding back on the far edge of the city.

The mass of them was so large that I could feel their presence coming closer without trying.

We were all going to die if we didn't flee.

CHAPTER TWENTY-SIX

I stabbed at the nearest enemy, determined to get back to the others and see if we could get the soldiers to safety and flee. At the same time, I wanted to pick up Capricia's body and bring her back with us. Kryos must have read my mind because as we got close, he picked her up and slung her over his shoulder.

It made it hit home that she wasn't alive anymore. We'd lost a good dragon and I would have to explain her death. A flash of memory stole my focus—the look on her face as she had been trying to talk and couldn't filled my head until a shadow catcher's tail caught me right in the midsection and knocked me back.

"Get your head together, Red." Kryos pushed me forward again.

Trying to do just that, I attacked another enemy, funneling my fury into every blow until it was dust and I could move on to the next one.

For a minute or so, the only thing in my head was the thought of killing more monsters. I yielded to it, letting

Kryos steer me and the sounds of battle wash over me like a balm in a storm.

The calm slaughter didn't last. The magic ran out in my armor and sword, and my ability to hurt the monsters before me went away with it. I was essentially useless. The connection to the isle of the ancestors was now so faint that I couldn't use it to recharge anything fast enough.

Kryos continued to urge me back to the others, where the groups had joined while we remained out on our own. The animals finally reached us as well, a mixture of all sorts of wildlife found across the country, from wolves and snakes to raccoons and more coyotes.

It made me wonder if there was any uncorrupted wildlife left in the US, but it also made our situation a thousand times worse.

I fought a little more, punching what I could and using up more of the armor magic, but at least doing some damage as I did. The sounds of vehicles and soldiers yelling suddenly grew louder, until the fighters I was with all turned toward the sound. Something rumbling was coming closer.

"Need a lift?" a familiar voice yelled.

Colonel Flint waved at me from what looked like the gunner position in a small armored vehicle not unlike a tank. It ran up on the sand as if it was the easiest terrain to drive on and slid to a halt, turning by ninety before it stopped. Someone threw open a back door that looked a bit like a hatch on a large cupboard and hands reached out to help me come aboard.

The roof was low, with a hole in the middle and a very special seat with nobody in it. I was ushered toward the seat, a set of headphones and a small mouth mic attached to the controls nearby. I noticed that Colonel Flint was wearing something similar, his eyes focused on the enemies in front of us.

Without really thinking or being conscious of the decision, I connected to the magic and charged the vehicle and any ammo it carried. Someone had already charged it to some degree, but it had been done in a hurry.

I added to the magic and perfected it, hoping it would help. And then I collapsed in the seat, hurting, crying, and shifting between grief and anger.

The soldiers had come to our rescue, and they'd used up everything I was charging for them in seconds in terms of ammo. It was noisy but somehow comforting. The human population had come to our rescue.

I didn't have to continue charging anything after a while. The other dragons around the battlefield that could control our magic started transferring the charge from our weapons to more and more tanks and the ammo of large guns.

As I watched, more and more of us ended up safely tucked into the backs of vehicles and surrounded by fresh soldiers. Still, the shadow catchers and their handlers kept coming. Above us, the demon continued to circle, the ever-present reminder that this battle wasn't over.

At some point, we passed close enough to my friends that Flick ran over to us and was helped up into the back of our tank. He came right over to me and pulled me into a hug.

I almost banged my head on the low ceiling, but I hugged him back and tried not to let any more tears fall.

"You did everything you could, and she died a hero's death. We'll honor that when all this is over," he said.

As he pulled away he shoved something into my hands. At first I didn't register what it was, and then I looked closer. It was the artifact.

"No clue what it does yet, but you might as well have it back. I can't fly it out of here." I put a hand on Flick's shoulder.

"Thank you for being willing to try and get it to safety. You took a huge risk having it off me."

Flick reached up and wiped one of my tears away. "And you take risks for us all the time. Now, come on, let's win this fight and show that demon that he can't take everything from us."

Hearing the confidence in Flick's voice despite the cuts and bruises all over him, the decay and damage that he'd also sustained, I felt him encourage me to my feet and to get involved in the fight again.

Not wanting to run the risk of losing the artifact, I strapped it to my wrist again. I connected to it automatically with no shield on that arm anymore. The artifact seemed to suck at my connection, but not in a bad way. It wanted me to give it some magic, and it was making that clear, but it wasn't forcing it, almost like a hungry child that was sitting there with the bowl and spoon ready and a hopeful look on their face. It was obvious what it wanted but it wasn't going to happen without some help from someone who knew how to get food.

There wasn't a lot of magic to be gained from anywhere at this point. All of us were running on close to empty, and what little we did have was being given to the soldiers to use while we rested. Despite that, I gave it some from my main source. The ancestors rescued me once again in this fight.

It drank it down, powering up in some way and making me feel instantly more awake and less tired. I still hurt, and I knew I had been in a fight, but I could think more clearly and I wanted to get to my feet and take stock again.

The bullets and tanks had torn through the animals and wildlife that had been set on us, as well as the shadow catchers. Some birds were still attacking, but the demon above appeared to be waiting us out.

With so many of us low or out of magic, I knew what he was waiting for. For all of us to be defenseless. I could still sense portals spitting more monsters out, and the demon was no doubt fully healed despite the extent of the damage I had done to him.

I needed more magic, and I needed it fast. We had to get those portals shut and the demon deterred. The artifact on my wrist didn't do much other than make me feel more buzzed, so I stopped putting magic into it and instead started to pump my sword full. Using the ancestors and pulling a tiny trickle from every dragon present, I started to fill up my sword, trying to work out how long it would take.

Despite gaining an advantage over the creatures pretty swiftly and making some of them turn and run, I felt as if nothing could win this fight still. Not unless I got a portal shut, or found some other way to hold the shadow catchers and corrupt creatures at bay.

As I thought this, our tank stopped and pointed ahead. We'd come full circle and were back by the original area we'd been protecting—the dry spring bed where I had set Lieutenant Douglas and asked him if he could help his people.

Several of the soldiers had stayed there, hoping that they wouldn't be attacked. They finally had some fruit from their labors. The machinery they were using broke through a section of more solid rock under the sandstone. Immediately, hot water gushed out, so hot steam rose off it, and the soldiers scrambled to get out of its way.

Relieved, I asked the soldiers to aim their tanks so they were on the inside edge of any moat this stream created. I felt lighter than I had since this fight had begun.

We traveled to the safer zone on the inside of the water as it spread fast around the outskirts of the city. At first it took a while to get anywhere. The ground seemed to drink it in, but after a while, it had soaked the area enough that the rest puddled and spread out.

It cut the tanks off from the shadow catchers as the body of water widened too far for them to travel across. They tried to go around, racing the water as it spread. Some of them succeeded, but they were quickly cut down. We stopped worrying about having the tanks charged, as no demons were getting close to them to do them any harm now. I sucked all the magic into me, recharging despite everyone else's needs.

When I felt refueled, I added to Neritas and then Flick, putting the magic back into dragons and pulling it from all equipment other than ammo. When there were four of us bearing plenty of magic, I started to give a little to the usual group who guarded me. All of them noticed they were suddenly feeling stronger again and looked my way, even if they were riding in different vehicles.

I heard the demon roar not long later, and hoped that he would give up the fight. The longer he waited now, the stronger I would grow. His army was also recovering, however, the portals helped him amass more monsters. We were gearing up for the final round.

Before he could decide to attack, I opened the door, leaped into the air, and transformed into a dragon again. *Fly with me,* I told every dragon I'd been powering up.

Not one of them hesitated. They all launched into the air and formed up around me. As a unit, I led them to the nearest portal and circled over it, out of reach of the shadow catchers coming from it. I pumped magic into it, using a little from all of us but more from me and the ancestors than anything else.

The portal shrank, but before it could close, what was left of the birds dove down on us, attacking. I rolled away, charging my scales and helping the others do the same, even though the majority of my group also had the ability to do so now.

More birds fell dead, but we also lost altitude, running the risk of being hit by a shadow catcher from below. Feeling sandwiched, I tried to think of something new to make the demon hesitate to send any more forces at us.

We can get the rest of these killed fast, Alitas suggested.

He zoomed away, keeping his wings out during the bird storm despite the possible damage to them. I followed, hoping he knew what he was doing.

It seemed he did. The birds raced to catch up, and having nowhere else to go, they followed us as Alitas smacked into the water and transformed back into a human. He sank under the surface as we all joined him.

The water was warm here, and it seemed to soothe the aches and pains I felt immediately. The birds followed us in, unable to slow in time. Many of them died on impact with the water—bird bones were far more brittle and their bodies weren't prepared for such impact. The rest of them were so corrupted that they reacted like the shadow catchers and exploded.

To both my surprise and relief, some of them seemed to clean up and become normal birds, free of the influence of the demon. They rose to the surface again and flew off, leaving the flock of corrupted birds severely depleted.

Our tactic didn't entirely finish them off, but it cleared the air enough that I felt confident going back to the surface and swimming to the shore. I was so tired that I almost tried to transform into a dragon in the water despite Ben's prior warning that I'd form with a lungful of water and kill myself.

I caught myself at the last minute and got out of the water and shook myself, water dripping from my clothing.

Before I could react, the demon catapulted toward me. I panicked, not ready for such an attack and still too wet to transform into a dragon. I connected to everything around me, searching for an answer as I started running.

Something activated in the artifact I was wearing, and where my feet had been running along sand I was running in midair.

It was a strange movement. Something in the artifact was raising me up and giving me lift, almost as if the air around us was being shifted and moved to give the sensation of being in the sky.

The demon roared again, as confused by this as I was. I used it to my advantage and lifted up and over, spinning in the sky and stabbing downward on the demon's back. I dug my sword in, just behind his neck, and hung on as he flew. The demon absorbed the magic in the sword but was also clearly hurt by it.

I realized this had given me the edge I needed to really fight back. The demon wasn't going to get away from me this time.

CHAPTER TWENTY-SEVEN

The demon rolled and shook, trying to do everything he could to lose me. I flew after him, pumping all my magic into keeping up and slashing at him. In the air, with several of my friends taking flight in dragon form and helping to hinder the demon, I was running circles around him.

Despite my best efforts, he was still healing himself. It was as if his magic was inexhaustible.

Eventually, I slowed. All the damage I was doing seemed to have no lasting impact, and my sword was running low on energy again.

I broke away, and it was as if he used a last burst of magic to put on speed and turn sharply. He got out from under me and broke away from Alitas as well. We could do nothing but watch him fly away or run the risk of using up all our magic and crashing hard in pursuit of him.

Land and let's get rid of as much of his army as possible. At least get these portals shut. We landed and for a minute watched the shadow catchers in disarray. It was as if they didn't know whether to fight this losing battle or flee.

Some of the handlers continued pushing their minions, but some opted to flee as well, or were told to do so by their master and commander. It was hard to tell.

I had enough magic left in me and my weapon that I wasn't ready to stop sending some of these forces to meet their maker, and headed for the nearest handler instead. This one was like a large tree, but covered in warts and fungus. I stabbed and hacked at it, flying around its head like a fly around a pile of crap.

It flailed its limbs at me, but I managed to dodge all of them and continue to hack at it. I felt as if I was an irritation, a very satisfying feeling.

Neritas and Flick joined me, landing and attacking from around its feet. This made it slower and more confused and allowed us to finish it off. By the time it was dead, many shadow catchers had come closer to help their controller, but they were instantly scrambled, their minds taking a while to fully adjust.

The soldiers and dragons killed many shadow catchers alike. I considered helping, but I couldn't do much. I was running low on energy again, the artifact using a fair amount and leaving me tired.

I landed in the middle of the battlefield and fought more shadow catchers, slaughtering them while they were confused and leaving anything bigger to the others. Although we were probably safe as a group, I couldn't bring myself to walk away from the fight entirely.

Alitas worked with Jace and some of the other powerful dragons to go back to closing the portals, and one of the handlers took the final one away, pulling it after him like a tugboat. I was going to have to fight this army again sometime, and I was passing up the chance to do something about it, but I could only do so much right now.

Exhausted and out of enemies in my immediate vicinity, I sat where I was. There was nothing graceful about it, and I wasn't taking in everything. It was the simple collapse of a body that had been pushed too hard and, now that it was safe, couldn't face anything else.

Before long, Neritas was behind me, also sitting there and taking my hand. Sometimes a shadow catcher came closer, but someone else killed it or chased it off, allowing me to rest.

I vaguely remembered people talking to me and asking me questions, but it was as if my mind had checked out. I answered as best I could and eventually got up as the citizens of the city returned. They were incredibly excited that their moat had been repaired.

With the return of the dragons also came more humans. The press wanted to talk to anyone who would respond. I knew if I continued to sit there I would be questioned, and I wasn't ready for that. With the magic no longer being drained from all of us and every possible source, the connections I had began to recover.

More soldiers turned up with provisions, like blankets and normal medical aid. I took some of the food they had and chowed down on the strange meal packets they were handing out. It helped me regain my ability to think and power anything, and I took out my pack and did as I always did after a battle—went around and healed those I could.

By the time I was done, I felt a lot better. I still hurt mercilessly where I had been injured, but I could push that sort of pain away. Nothing more could be done to repair me. At least not with magic.

The hardest thing to do by far was look upon the dead form of my captain of the guard and figure out the best way to handle her funeral. Capricia was permanently gone from my world, and the world was the worse for losing her. I would take her body back to Detaris.

"I'm sorry that you lost someone," Lieutenant Douglas said as he came up to me again. I'd been past him once already, healing him on my way to heal others. He'd not been hurt badly. The soldiers had been fortunate enough to have been protected for most of the battle.

"She was a pain in the ass at times, but she had a warrior's heart and she protected anyone who needed it." As I said the words, I thought of the one time she hadn't actually protected me, but I let it slide. I hadn't needed her protection, not really. I just hadn't wanted to fight and defend myself.

Sometimes I wondered if she had planned my journey too. After I'd found out that my parents had deliberately put me, a dragon, into the human child system to grow up, it made me wonder if other things in my life hadn't been planned as an exercise to help me grow.

The thought was cynical, and I pushed it away to consider my options now. I'd gained an artifact and made this city a lot more defensible again with the help of the US Army. In a lot of ways, it should have been considered a successful mission, but it didn't entirely feel like one.

I was about to go to my friends and the others from Detaris to suggest we leave and let the residents and soldiers from closer around here rebuild and clean up, when Ben came up to me.

"Well done, Scarlet. I think Anthony would be very proud of you in this moment. You've shown that you can not only lead our people but that you're willing to do what it takes, risk yourself above others, and fight until the very end."

I shook my head, feeling tears threaten to fall again. My gaze traveled to Capricia's dead form, now lying in the back of a tank and covered up. He followed it and sighed.

"Do I need to tell you that her death isn't your fault?" Ben asked.

I shook my head, not blaming myself so much as the demon and everything that led to him escaping. I hadn't been perfect in trying to get the gate repaired, and many others had gotten in the way of me dealing with it. Capricia's death was a consequence of a very complicated set of events. None of them were a direct cause, even if I wanted to blame myself.

"I do know that if we go after any more artifacts, we need a lot more magic and preparation."

"And a lot more dragons." Ben shrugged and tried to smile at me as if he had made a joke.

"Or soldiers," Douglas offered, showing he had heard a lot of the conversation. "Though I can't even begin to pretend to understand how any of your fancy tech works."

"That's why they call it magic, Lieutenant," Colonel Flint said as he joined us.

"Anything sufficiently advanced appears to be magic to those who don't understand it?" Douglas raised an eyebrow as he looked at his superior.

"Exactly that. And I don't understand it, but I'm very grateful it works. The general is asking if we'd all return to Detaris and the army camp there for a debrief and to rest and recharge. Says there's some more US personnel on their way to assist the dragons with rebuilding their city, especially in getting that spring to stick around and act as a moat or whatever it needs to be."

I shook the colonel's hand and thanked him. Even if he had been following orders, he had turned up right when we needed him and I would always be grateful.

Before I had finished, Bartholomew approached me. He looked paler than when I had seen him last, although I hadn't thought that was possible at the time.

"You are indeed the queen of all dragons. None of us want to keep you when we know that you are hurting, but you have saved us this day and given us a hope for our city's future that we haven't had in years. Thank you for all you've done. Words aren't enough."

I got the impression that he'd have continued expressing his gratitude for hours in various ways if the press hadn't chosen to take that moment to record me and ask me questions again. I hadn't planned on talking to them about anything, but it gave me a way out of the current conversation and something to do until my dragons were strong enough to leave.

"Is it true? Did you almost die today?" the first reporter asked. This was going to be an awkward interview and I wasn't going to like it.

I shrugged and walked away. I was already put off learning and adapting to being in the human world. I kept moving, done talking to everybody, until Neritas took my hand again and led me away from everyone else.

"Are you going to give me another piece of wisdom or advice based on what you think I need after that crazy battle that consumed us both?" I asked.

He shook his head. "No. I planned on asking you if there was anything I could do to help, but I meant more in a logistics, get-everyone-where-they-need-to-go sort of way."

I didn't have a clue and expressed as much, but I appreciated the sentiment. He wasn't making demands of me or expecting anything.

"We need more dragons," I told him, well aware that I was repeating what someone else had said to me.

"You're not wrong, but they're not going to be easy to find, especially with the media plastering the news of a dragon dying all over the news."

"We're going to need to give them something else to talk about, then. Something more positive."

Neritas tipped his head to the side as he considered the problem.

"I know the elders aren't going to like it, but what if we invited them to Detaris? It's your city and it would be a different focus point. Show them everything we can do and how much we want to protect everyone. I also think it's time to come clean that we can also control the same magic as you."

I nodded. I had considered what it might do for everyone thinking about being able to mix magics and fight back. It would take training, but it would mean that anyone could be powerful in battle. Or do other things that interested them with the power. It had a lot of scope.

Neritas was right. We couldn't hide it any longer. When the secret that dragons existed had come out, everyone also needed to know that we were equals. Some of us had a preference for using our magic in different ways, but everyone could combine magics.

I hoped it would bring us together.

CHAPTER TWENTY-EIGHT

As the first political person to ever be close, once she stepped inside the shield of Detaris and could see the city for the first time, Dinah gasped and looked around as if something was a trick.

"This is beautiful." She came closer to me, still staring at everything in wonder. I wasn't sure if she meant the dragons flying around everywhere or the city and its architecture, but I smiled as if it was a compliment that I was grateful to receive.

My warmth brought her over in my direction as we waited for everyone else to arrive. We were playing hosts to almost a hundred different dignitaries from various countries and I wanted Detaris to appear in the best possible light.

It felt scary to have them in the city, but as everyone had agreed, we needed more allies. This time around, the dragons alone weren't powerful enough to defeat the demon, especially as he had three of the artifacts that had been used to defeat it the first time.

Having yet another large fight out in public view a few days earlier had made the world more interested in us.

While some of the battle in Havilah had unfolded behind its shield, the device had quickly failed, hit by a shadow catcher that had gone straight for it and hit it hard, no doubt with a handler controlling them. The world had seen most of it.

I had got back to Detaris two days before them to find videos and news reports the world over about the fight we had won in a combined effort with the soldiers. Although it showed many of us fighting, it was clear from the sentiment expressed on several of the news sites that I was being considered a superhero of sorts.

Many of the clips were of me and the way I had stood alone and faced the demon. It had been strange to watch him send me flying as we fought on and hurt each other, the damage done enough to kill many humans. Of course, I had been able to heal, and he could do enough damage in one strike that Capricia had died. The difference between our outcomes had made me look more powerful.

Inviting some politicians and reporters to Detaris was meant to be a way to show them that I was just another dragon, as well as get us help in the future. It was also to squash the one other concern we had, which was the way things were being reported.

Everyone was calling us secretive and expressing fears that we could be hiding anything in our cities. This would hopefully show that we weren't and that other than our war with the demon, we were a very peaceful race.

As the reporters showed up next, they pulled out video cameras and recorded everything, getting footage of the dragons swooping around the city and the way the whole thing was hidden on one side of the shield and not on the other.

"You call it a shield, right?" one of the journalists asked as he came closer.

I nodded. "Yes, although it's partially a misnomer. It doesn't keep any attacks out, only hides us. For a very long time that has been enough."

As I spoke, I wondered about the downside of being so honest about what we were capable of. Humanity wasn't known for being compassionate to those who were different, especially when scared. But if we never appeared to be a threat, despite our strength, then perhaps harmony could be secured from the beginning.

Some of the soldiers, curious to be here and see it, had asked to come to the city at the same time. It would show us working together well, so I had quickly agreed.

I greeted everyone personally, trying to focus on just being there until everyone had arrived and I could let the elders take over and conduct a tour. As before, a very precise route had been chosen and the group was actually split into three so the city could accommodate that many new people all at once. Because most of the dragons could fly and there were less than a thousand of us in the city, it wasn't easy to add a hundred who couldn't fly around between places.

With more than one group, I moved between them, flying from one to the other at opportune moments. I had rehearsed these changes in my head, wanting to give the groups a similar amount of my time throughout the day.

It appeared to go well. The questions they asked were

sometimes tough and to the point, but I'd gone over what to say to some of them with Alitas the previous day and I felt as if I answered the majority of them well. Of course, I wouldn't know until we saw how our visitors reacted on their news later and in any further politics between all of us.

The day slipped by, and all the while I wondered what the demon was doing. Nothing had been seen of him again for several days now and we had made no more progress with finding another definite city that held an artifact. There were a few possibilities, and we had asked some dragons to check their vault areas very carefully.

Nothing had come to light yet, though.

With no demon attacks and nothing new from our end, it was the perfect moment to be diplomatic, but I was as eager to see them all leave again, nerves settling in when I remembered what I had agreed to do afterward.

I was also still exhausted. The fight had drained me of magical energy and I was still recovering. The connection to the ancestors had mostly gotten back to full strength, but that wasn't something I wanted to test further right now.

All I wanted to do was sleep, but instead, as the visitors began to leave, their tour and interviews over, I had to go to the elders' chambers to talk about this and everything else the city needed to know.

"Keep all the doors open," I said as I landed.

I got raised eyebrows from some of the elders and my mother, but I knew others were aware of what I was about to say. They had all come to the meeting so they could back me up and show the truth of my words if it wasn't believed by everyone.

I went to my throne and sat on it. I didn't feel entirely comfortable under that many eyes, but this was where I needed to be for this announcement.

While everyone was still settling into their positions and adjusting back to an all-dragon meeting, I kept to polite formalities, thanking everyone for the day and going over minor city details.

I tried not to take too long on it before I got to my main point.

"Now, to the most important reason you are all here. I want to apologize with all my heart for not revealing it sooner, and also for the lies those who have sat here in the past have used to shroud this subject."

As I paused, I looked around the room. The elders had given me their full attention already, as had everyone who knew. Neritas and Flick showed subtle signs of nerves as well. The rest of their audience reacted to my words, however. From this point onward they would hang onto my every word.

"As many of you know, with the break in line to the throne and the choice my father made of hiding me among humans and not raising me here, there's a lot I was never told about being a red dragon or what was going on. It's also become clear to the elders and many of the dragons around me that at some point in our history, they deliberately chose to repress what was known about the demon, what we could do to protect ourselves, and how important certain elements of our race are."

There were nods at this, especially from the elders. It

was no secret, but it was the foundation for the news I was about to give them. Again I paused, trying to phrase this next part the right way.

"In the last few months, we began to learn of something else that had been repressed. A knowledge that is likely to have been deliberately kept from all dragons to increase the power of the throne. I took this knowledge to my closest advisers, and we verified it, tested it, and started to explain it and teach it to select others. One of those was Capricia, and it was one of the reasons she stood with me in battle two days ago. I tell you all now to honor what she gave, her memory, and how she never gave up."

Tears stung my eyes again as my words tumbled out and went in a direction I hadn't intended.

"When we perform the life ceremony for Capricia later today, I want you all to know how much she gave for this city, how well she fought, and what she was learning with the intention of passing it on. The magic that you were told was exclusive to my color. The ability to combine our magics, connect us all and feed it into our weapons, shields, and armor is something we can all learn to do. My ancestors kept it from you for reasons I will never know, but now that I know it, I cannot keep it to myself any longer."

I'd expected gasps at my confession, angry accusations, or something noisy in some way. But instead, I was met with a silence so deep that I almost wondered if I had gone momentarily deaf.

"And you're sure of this?" Brenta asked.

I looked at Neritas and nodded. He stepped forward.

"I was the first person Scarlet taught to use the same

ability—purely to test this theory. I've been assisting her in battle, and I taught Capricia and Jace, and have begun teaching Jared as well. This is truly something that we can all do, although, like any of our magics, it is harder for some than others."

Finally the murmuring started as the population talked about it.

"As I have already said, I can only give you my apology that this wasn't shared with you sooner. I had no idea anything like this was possible until a few months ago, and at first, we assumed Neritas must have red ancestry. Only when we discovered that he didn't, and understood that we could teach anyone, did we realize what a lie had been told." I got up off the throne and bowed to the elders and the people.

I had no desire to continue our meeting after this revelation. They weren't going to want to talk about other subjects and I wasn't going to force them to. I didn't rush off, however. I was going to answer questions, demonstrate if need be, and stick around until the sun set and it was time to say goodbye to Capricia.

Although I tried not to think about the latter, I knew her death was tied up in all of this. She had flown to my side to protect me, but she had also been funneling magic through herself and fighting the demon head-on. I wasn't responsible for her death, but I had played a part in her final moments.

To my surprise, the city and its inhabitants were surprisingly understanding, especially the elders and Brenta.

"This doesn't ring false—that a red dragon in the past

had kept this from us. The mistrust between the colors has formed for a reason. But it is the first time I have felt sure that period of our history is over. Thank you, Scarlet, for giving us back the knowledge you have gained in your time here and for never failing to look out for your fellow dragons." Brenta took my hand and gave it a squeeze before shuffling off.

My mouth fell open long enough that I had to close it with a snap of my jaws. Of everyone, I had expected her to be the most angry and the one most likely to accuse me of also covering it up, even with the lie detector in the floor of the chamber.

As Neritas and Flick took over taking the questions and showing people what I meant, I allowed myself to slip back and prepare for the ceremony. I had agreed to preside over it as both Capricia's leader and friend, and I wanted her to have the best sendoff I could give her.

She had given everything in service to the world and tried to keep it safe. I wanted to honor that.

EPILOGUE

It felt strange to be in the library again after so many days of avoiding it. I hadn't felt as if I could go back to it after Capricia had died. Partially because finding Havilah had happened here, and it ultimately led to her death, but partially because I knew Ben had hit dead end after dead end and I didn't want to pressure him.

Capricia was the second dragon we had lost to this fight with the demon and his minions, and I knew Ben felt the first loss most keenly. It had been over a year, but Anthony had meant a lot to him, and I never wanted to be insensitive to that.

I had to move on and fight, however. We needed to know where the next artifact might be.

As Ben came out from the stacks of books and noticed me, I put a plate of food down on the table for him. He smiled at me, though the light didn't quite reach his eyes, and gave me a hug.

"I'm glad you popped in. I think I might have been in

here alone a little too long." He pulled away and reached for the plate.

Although I was curious about what he meant, I didn't push for an explanation. He needed to eat and I would rather he focused on that.

I sat opposite him and waited, looking over the books he had left out. There were more books on the various rulers, maps of the cities, and histories of all sorts lying out. Some of them were open to possibly relevant pages, and many had little paper bookmarks sticking out of them to note other references.

"I know it's a mess in here. Don't tell our head librarian," he added when his plate of food was mostly gone.

"Your secrets are always safe with me," I replied. He had kept mine many times.

It earned me another grin before he sat back and studied me. "I'm not making progress. I know where the cities might be, but... Either the rulers have no idea that they might have a treasure under their city, or..."

"Entirely possible," I replied when he paused.

"Or they're lying to me. And I have absolutely no idea why they might be, other than the demon has got to them somehow."

Ben's words sent a chill through me as I realized that he was serious and this was what he had been referring to by being in here too long.

"How sure are you?" I leaned in a little closer and gave Ben my full attention.

"At this point, it's all I've got to go on. I'm ninety-nine percent sure there is an artifact in a city near New York. But the elders there are telling me that it's not possible and has never been possible." He shrugged, clearly not wanting to accuse them fully.

"Could it be that they genuinely believe they don't have it?" I asked.

"Maybe, but I suggested that you visit and check it out anyway. Said that you had ways of finding these things even if they're lost."

"And they didn't like that?"

"They didn't like that one bit." The seriousness of his tone said everything I needed to know. He thought they were lying and he thought I should do something about it.

"Sounds like they need a surprise visit from their queen and all her honor guards." I nodded and stood, ready to start planning it.

Ben also got up. He closed several of the books. "I think you're going to need an army. This city rivals Detaris in size and population. And they're not going to let you in without a fuss."

I exhaled and considered his words. If I had to fight misguided dragons to get the artifacts, this war was going to take on a whole new level of difficulty.

"Talk us through everything so we can be sure, and we'll make a plan."

Ben grinned and gave my hand a squeeze. "I was hoping you'd say that. You come up with the best plans."

His vote of confidence made me feel better as we headed back to the royal tower and took several books with us. I had managed to defeat the demon so well in our last battle that no one had heard from him in a week, but it had been one battle. The war was just beginning.

THE STORY CONTINUES

The story continues with book eight, *Dragon Unveiling*, available at Amazon.

Claim your copy today!

ACKNOWLEDGMENTS

For me, the real fun part of any series I write is beginning the first book in the final trilogy of a series. In this case, book seven of nine. I have always found it naturally easier to write in trilogies when it comes to plot arcs and then layering that up in trilogies and then more threes. I don't know if it's because of the structure of a three act play, or something else at work, but it works for me.

This book has been no different although it also felt as if it had a mind of its own at points. I am grateful for each one of you who have read this far, however. Thank you for all the support you've shown me and all the messages and emails you've sent. You're all awesome.

To LMBPN and all the wonderful people who work on my books, including, Robin, Steve, Kelly, Grace, Jacqui, Tracey and anyone I've not mentioned by name because we don't talk as much.

To Bryan for caring for me and keeping me going with snacks and drinks when I'm trying to get the words out and make this somehow coherent.

And to my two tiny humans. You bring a lot of laughter and light to my life, even if you also stress me out and make me feel crazy sometimes. You remind me what I work hard for and why this world is worth fighting for.

To Andrew, Anne-Mhairi, Bear, David and Clare.

You're on the journey of life with me and I'm grateful for every part you play in my life and that of my family. I couldn't do this without you all.

And last, but not least, to God. I'm not a perfect person, but I'm trying to be like your son. Not what people say he is, or what they think he is, but who he really is. His heart was full of love and for that I am always thankful.

ABOUT THE AUTHOR

Jess is in the process of changing her name. She's been through a difficult year that leaves her wanting a fresh start and a chance to be the person she's always meant to be. Over the next little while all her books will be moving to Talia Beckett and you'll find all future releases under this author name.

Talia was born in the quaint village of Woodbridge in the UK, has spent some of her childhood in the States and now resides near the beautiful Roman city of Bath. She lives with her two tiny humans (one boy and one girl) and near an amazing group of friends who support her career and life choices.

During her still relatively short life Talia has displayed an innate curiosity for learning new things and has therefore studied many subjects, from maths and the sciences, to history and drama. Talia now works full time as a writer and mummy, incorporating many of the subjects she has an interest in within her plots and characters.

When she's not busy with work and keeping her tiny humans alive she can often be found with friends, playing with miniature characters, dice and pieces of paper covered in funny stats and notes about fictional adventures her figures have been on.

You can find out more about the author and her

upcoming projects by joining her on facebook, by watching her live D&D streams, or emailing her via tali-abeckettwriter@gmail.com. Talia loves hearing from a happy fan so please do get in touch!

Talia is also opening up her discord for fans to come chat about what she's up to, and see a few sneak peaks of future work. There's also a chance to become one of her beta readers. If you'd like to check that out you can do so here.

CONNECT WITH THE AUTHOR

Connect with Talia

Mailing list sign up
Facebook group.
Discord group
Actual play D&D stream: Twitch or Youtube
Email address: contact me here.

BOOKS BY JESS MOUNTIFIELD / TALIA BECKETT

Already published

Urban Fantasy

Dragon of Shadow and Air:

Air Bound

Shadow Sworn

Dragon Souled

Earth Bound

Night Sworn

Dryad Souled

Water Bound

Day Sworn

Pegasus Souled

Fire Bound

Light Sworn

Phoenix Souled

Dragon Apparent:

Dragon Missing

Dragon Seeking

Dragon Revealed

Dragon Rising

Dragon Defying
Dragon Crowned
Dragon Defending

Time of the Dragon (with Andrew Bellingham):
Dragon's Code
Dragon's Inquisition
Dragon's Redemption
Dragon's Revolt
Dragon's Summit
Dragon's Reckoning

Fantasy
Tales of Ethanar:
Wandering to Belong (Tale 1)
Innocent Hearts (Tale 2 & 3)
For Such a Time as This (Tale 4)
A Fire's Sacrifice (Tale 5)

Winter Series:
The Hope of Winter (Tale 6.05)
The Fire of Winter (Tale 6.1)

Guild of the Eternal Flame:
Wayfarer's Sanctuary
Protector's Secret

Healer's Oath

Other Fantasy:
The Initiate (under Holly Lujah)

Writing with Dawn Chapman:
Jessica's Challenge (#5 in the Puatera Online series)
Dahlia's Shadow (#6 in the Puatera Online series)
Lila's Revenge (#7 in the Puatera Online series)

Sci-Fi:

Fringe Colonies:
Alliance

Haven

Rebellion

Rebirth

Reclamation

Star Trail:
Hunted

Sherdan series:
Sherdan's Prophecy

Sherdan's Legacy

Sherdan's Country

Sherdan's Road (A short story in the anthology 'The End of the Road')

The Slave Who'd Never Been Kissed (A short in the charity anthology 'Imaginings')

New Beginnings

Santa's Little Space Pirate

In the multi-author Adamanta series:

Episode 1 – Adamanta

Episode 3 – Excelsior

Episode 8 – Phoenix

Episode 13 – New Contacts

Episode 17 – Sacrifice

Other:

Clues, Claws and Christmas

Non-Fic:

How to Write Lots, and Get Sh*t Done: the Art of Not Being a Flake

[Find purchase links here](#)

Coming soon:

Urban Fantasy:

Dragon Apparent:

Dragon Unveiling

Dragon Transcended

Time of the Dragon (with Andrew Bellingham):

Dragon's Exodus

Fantasy:

(Tales of Ethanar):

The Pursuit of Winter (#2 in the Winter series, Tale 6.2)

Books under Amelia Price

Mycroft Holmes Adventures:

The Hundred Year Wait

The Unexpected Coincidence

The Invisible Amateur

The Female Charm

The Reluctant Knight

The Ambitious Orphan

The Unconventional Honeymoon Gift

The Family Reunion

The Immortal Problem

The Unremarkable Assistant

Coming soon:

Mycroft 11

OTHER BOOKS FROM LMBPN
PUBLISHING

Sign up for the LMBPN email list to be notified of new releases and special deals!

https://lmbpn.com/email/

For a complete list of books by LMBPN please visit:

https://lmbpn.com/books-by-lmbpn-publishing/

www.ingramcontent.com/pod-product-compliance
Lightning Source LLC
LaVergne TN
LVHW041223080526
838199LV00083B/2403